Julia shivered, hal
half because the ~~temperature had~~
dropped precipitously.

Frank noticed, but she had the feeling he noticed everything about her. "Go upstairs to the master suite where I'm staying. There should be a sweater in the closet. I'll bring these blankets downstairs."

Back to her fantasy room. She ducked in and grabbed a yellow fleece pullover that made her look like a hazard sign.

Returning downstairs, she noticed Frank had set the blankets on the big leather couch in front of the fireplace and was eyeing the iron firewood rack. "We don't have much wood inside. I'll go to the shed in back to bring more in."

"Do you need me to help?"

He laughed. "You're asking a Portuguese man if he wants a woman to help him with heavy lifting? Remember where you are."

"Hmmph." As if she could forget the near castle they were in. "Would you like me to cook or clean something while you do all the manly work around here?"

He gave her a long look up and down her body. "You▨▨▨▨▨▨▨▨▨▨▨▨nly worl▨▨▨▨▨▨▨▨▨▨▨▨the kitch▨

ROYALLY CLAIMED

BY
MARIE DONOVAN

MILLS & BOON

First published in Great Britain 2013
by Mills & Boon, an imprint of Harlequin (UK) Limited,
Eton House, 18-24 Paradise Road, Richmond, Surrey TW9 1SR

© Marie Donovan 2011

ISBN: 978 0 263 90513 7

30-0713

Harlequin (UK) policy is to use papers that are natural, renewable and recyclable products and made from wood grown in sustainable forests. The logging and manufacturing processes conform to the legal environmental regulations of the country of origin.

by Blackprint CPI, Barcelona

Marie Donovan is a Chicago-area native who got her fill of tragedies and unhappy endings by majoring in opera/vocal performance and Spanish literature. As an antidote to all that gloom, she read romance novels voraciously throughout college and graduate school.

Donovan worked for a large suburban public library for ten years as both a cataloguer and a bilingual Spanish story-time presenter. She graduated magna cum laude with two bachelor's degrees from a Midwestern liberal arts university and speaks six languages. She enjoys reading, gardening and yoga.

Please visit the author's website at www.mariedonovan.com.

To all my English teachers in high school, my Spanish, German and French teachers and professors, and to the little old *signora* at the language school, who taught me just enough Italian to be dangerous. I couldn't have written these books and the previous seven without you. Many thanks, in whatever language you choose.

1

JULIA COOPER SQUEEZED her eyes shut and blinked hard a few times as she sat at a small café table. She couldn't have seen what she'd thought at first. Ever since her concussion, she didn't quite trust how her optic nerve was shooting messages back to her cerebral cortex. Misbehaving brain. Had to be playing tricks on her.

Even so, her heart still pounded as the man walked down the cobblestone street. He chatted with an older man, hands moving animatedly. Darned if he didn't look like Frank, at least from the back, black hair curling over his collar as if he'd forgotten to get a haircut. The man disappeared around a corner before she saw his face. Of course, all the men on this Azorean island of São Miguel, St. Michael's island, were dark, their sunny Portuguese heritage transplanted to a cool and misty string of rocks in the middle of the North Atlantic. Although the chain of islands stretched almost four hundred miles from end to end, São Miguel, the largest, was less than three hundred square miles in area according to her father, a huge geography buff.

Did the Azorean men ever have some ancestral

longing for the hot, dry mainland, she wondered idly. A remnant of mitochondrial DNA passed from their mothers that made them crave the juice of blood oranges running down their chins as the Mediterranean sun beat on their heads?

She shook her head—cautiously, though. Fanciful thoughts for a decidedly unfanciful woman. Perhaps she was experiencing one of those moments that the poets described, where magic and reality entwined, the hazy time between waking and sleeping when you dreamed strange things—or were they dreams?

And what was reality? Was it that past life of hers in Boston, that world of white fluorescent, green scrubs and red blood? Blood and oranges. Blood oranges. She had a sudden craving for citrus, a craving for sun.

Or was it a Vitamin C deficiency? Ah, there was her normal nature asserting itself. She laughed softly, not wishing to appear as flaky on the outside as she sometimes felt on the inside.

It was normal, they had assured her. Normal, she scoffed. As if anything that had happened to her could be called normal.

But she was here, not just in the Azores, but *here* here, alive and breathing. Still on this earth. And that was something. What, she couldn't exactly say.

Frank, the recesses of her mind whispered to her. *Francisco,* they insisted. And that was what she had feared, coming back here—the insistence of her thoughts. Not just her thoughts, her emotions.

Enough. Julia set her coffee cup down with a resolute clink and stood. Good, no more dizziness today. But she was a bit tired. Fatigue is your body reminding you to rest. She had learned that in nursing school and grad school, but mostly ignored it. Her reserves were much lower now than back then.

Home again, home again. She picked her way along the uneven street, stopping to peer into store windows. Around her, friends greeted each other with affectionate cheek kisses, talking animatedly in the local Azorean dialect. She remembered a couple of words from when she was a child but not enough to understand their conversation.

Julia just let the noise wash over her and bought an English-language newspaper for her dad and a German candy bar her mother enjoyed. She climbed a small hill to her parents' apartment in a renovated old stone farmhouse, brushing her dark curly hair out of her face in the ever-present ocean breeze.

She could use a good trim. Her hair was the type that grew bigger, rather than longer, and the humidity was poufing her hair into a dark facsimile of a clown wig. Maybe she'd ask around to see if any of the island beauty shops could handle the daunting task.

She waved to their landlord, *Senhor* de Sousa, who offered her fresh berries. He chatted away to her in a mix of English and Portuguese. She nodded and smiled and couldn't help contrasting it with her own condo building, where she knew her next-door neighbors only by sight and not by name.

She gracefully withdrew from what looked to be a rather involved conversation and climbed the steps to the apartment.

Instead of seeing her parents sharing a quiet cup of coffee, they were in a tizzy. Her mother paced back and forth, listening intently to the phone while her dad clicked away on the laptop. "If we book now, we can get a flight out later this afternoon," he called.

Mother made an impatient gesture and then caught sight of Julia. "Oh, thank goodness. Here, my daughter is a nurse. Tell her what's going on." She shoved the phone at Julia, who grabbed it.

"Who's sick?" she hissed.

"Your great aunt Elva and uncle Paul."

Julia winced. Aunt Elva and Uncle Paul were her favorite relatives. "Hello?" Unfortunately, she was speaking to a hospital social worker. Her aunt and uncle had been driving along minding their own business when a truck plowed into their sedate sedan. Aunt Elva had bruised ribs and a broken arm, needing pins put in to stabilize the fracture. Uncle Paul had a broken leg but wouldn't require surgery as long as he kept off his feet. "No head injuries or broken hips, pelvises, nothing like that?"

The social worker assured her that wasn't the case and Julia quickly explained to her mom and dad. Broken hips and pelvises were almost a death sentence for the elderly, few recovering well from that injury.

Julia made a few notes on the paper that her mother shoved at her. They were in a hospital in the Boston suburbs, one with a good reputation for patching people up. She told the social worker someone would be there in a couple days when they were released and got the direct number for their hospital rooms to call later. She hung up. "So when are we going?"

Dad looked up from the laptop, peering over his half-moon reading glasses. "We can get a flight out tomorrow morning and be in Boston in under five hours." Thanks to the large Azorean community in Boston, direct flights were pretty frequent, by Azorean standards.

Her mother twisted her hands together. "But what will we do about Julia?"

"What do you mean? You don't need to do anything about me. I'm coming with you. Aunt Elva and Uncle Paul won't stay in the hospital for very long. When they go home, they'll need nursing care, and I am a nurse. A nurse practitioner, even."

Her dad shook his head. "They need somebody who can help them up and down to the bathroom, move them around in bed. Basic nursing assistant skills. Brute strength that you don't have. You fall over if you stand up too fast."

"Dad!" He had all the tact of a bull from one of the local ranches.

As usual, her mother stepped in to smooth Dad's bluntness. "I know you would do anything to help, but Julia, honey, you're not strong enough right now."

Great. Her parents thought she was as much an invalid as her poor aunt and uncle. At least she could make it to the bathroom on her own.

"We want you to come back with us," her mother continued. "You can sleep on the pullout couch at their apartment."

Julia winced. Aunt Elva and Uncle Paul had a modest two-bedroom apartment, big enough for them, but a tight squeeze for five adults plus whatever nursing staff they needed.

Her dad raised his eyebrows. "Come on, Evelyn, you know we're going to be packed in like sardines, anyway. And what is Julia going to do all day with us old folks? Watch game shows and soap operas?"

No need to watch soap operas, her life had been one for quite a while.

"We can get you set up at your condo, and then you can come spend the day with us!" her mother exclaimed with a sudden bright idea.

Julia caught Dad's sympathetic gaze. He knew she would be climbing the walls within a few days. At least it was spring in Boston, although mid-April was a toss-up with the real possibility of snow. "No," she said impulsively, "I'll stay here."

"What? No, you can't," Mother protested. "By yourself?"

It sounded better the longer she thought about it. Go back to gray, cloudy Boston, bundle up in her down parka and stagger around in the slush or stay here in the sunny green Azores and eat fresh oranges from the trees? "I'm doing much better." Julia ticked off the points on her fingers. "I haven't had a bad headache in the past week, I'm not dizzy very often, and *Senhor* de Sousa can help with anything I may need. He would do that anyway."

"Oh…" Mother fretted. "I would worry so, with you so far away."

Dad unexpectedly came to her rescue. "Evelyn, we'd be only four hours away by plane. The girl is getting stronger and we can't be hovering over her like a helicopter. She'd be more likely to have a nervous breakdown than a relapse with us."

"Thanks, Dad."

He pointed a thick finger at her. "But we expect you to have some common sense. Carry your cell phone with you and stay away from cliffs and those rodeos they call bullfights around here."

"And call Dr. da Silva if you start feeling funny." Her mother rummaged in the papers on the table. "Here's his number. But I don't know…"

"I'll be fine," she assured her mother. "I'm just not… ready to go back to Boston yet."

"Understood," Dad said. "But just say the word and I'll hop a flight back to São Miguel to collect you."

"Thanks." She smiled at him. Master Sergeant Robert Cooper, United States Air Force (ret.), was an expert at hopping flights and collecting people.

The rest of the evening was spent helping her parents pack, mostly her mother since Dad could pack anything into a small duffel bag and proclaim himself well supplied.

When Julia brushed her teeth that night, the memory of that dark-haired man in the plaza popped to mind. Was she staying behind just in case he was Frank? And what on earth would she do if it was her former lover? Her first lover, she mentally corrected herself. The first man she'd loved.

FRANCISCO DUARTE DAS Aguas Santas stared at a wall of paint chips until spots formed in front of his eyes. Yes, he knew the villa needed a fresh coat of paint, but why was he the one picking out colors? He glanced at Benedito, whose dark brown eyes were rheumy with age. Ah, that was why he was the one picking out colors. He supposed his mother or one of his sisters could have done it, but he had offered to get the villa ready for Stefania's honeymoon and this was little enough he could do for her.

"What do you think, Benedito? What color for the

kitchen walls? Does that yellow have too much green in it?"

The old man looked at him as if he had grown two heads, or more likely, lost both testicles. "Don Franco, this is a job for women. Women choose paint, men paint it on the walls. We are not supposed to know these kinds of things. And why do you think yellow has green in it? Yellow is yellow, green is green."

Frank grunted. "We don't have any women handy."

"And whose fault is that? I am not a young, handsome duke who owns a huge ranch in Portugal and a private island here in the Azores. No, I am a poor, ugly old man whose devoted wife is far away."

"And she's probably glad to have you several thousand miles away, you old reprobate."

"She is grateful for the rest. I am an insatiable man," Benedito leered.

Frank rolled his eyes but didn't doubt the bandy-legged old coot. After lifetimes of hard manual labor and plenty of olive oil and red wine, elderly Portuguese men were as hearty as men half their age.

"You should be so insatiable," Benedito scolded him. An elderly lady picking out pink chips the color of a stomach remedy gave them an interested look.

Frank ducked around to the next aisle, filled with bolts and screws. Benedito followed him. "Enough about my personal life. Besides, I am thinking of asking Paulinha to start accompanying me to social functions."

Benedito made a phlegmy sound of dismay. "Don Franco, you know that is as good as becoming engaged to her. She has been chasing you since she was old enough to walk."

Frank shrugged. Paulinha was his sister's best friend

and had been unofficially matched with him, like the princes of Portugal who became engaged to French princesses at the age of six. A dynastic merger, rather than a matter of love. "I am thirty. It is past time for me to settle down." He'd had enough of the hardware section and turned into the garden aisle. Everything grew well in the fertile, volcanic soil here, so all they had to do was weed and trim the grounds.

"If you had gone wild like some of the other lazy noblemen, drinking, womanizing and acting like an idiot, then I would welcome you settling down. But you have never done anything to settle down *from*." Benedito shook his head. "Bah, you have wasted your youth."

"What, working on the family estate with you, your wife, my mother and four younger sisters all looking over my shoulder?" Once he was finished with his education, he'd returned home to the family estate, or *fazenda,* as it was called in Portuguese. The fazenda, named Aguas Santas after the natural spring's "holy waters" that bubbled up in the churchyard fountain, was a huge outfit on the Portuguese mainland with several farms, ranches and vineyards. His mother, the Dowager Duchess, still lived there in a smaller house on the property. Two of his sisters and their families lived nearby and the other two were at university in London and Lisbon, respectively.

"I've barely been alone to take a coffee break, much less waste my youth. Besides, isn't that the speech the disappointed father gives to a dissolute son who wanders back after blowing all his money on wine, women and song?"

Benedito grabbed his wallet, yanking out a handful of euros. "Here, take my money and waste it. Waste it on wine, women and song. You are like the virgin who chooses the convent before she can experience life."

"Ah…" Frank pushed the money away in disgust and Benedito shook it at him. "Stop shoving your money at me."

A middle-aged male clerk walked around the corner, eyeing them with interest. Frank groaned and grabbed some seeds. "No, Ben, you don't have to pay for these, I'll pay."

Disappointed, the clerk wandered away. Benedito let out a wheezing laugh. "If only you were here with a beautiful lady, he wouldn't have gotten the wrong idea."

Frank rolled his eyes. Maybe he could text his sisters for some paint ideas. "Come on, old man, let's get some coffee."

"Ah, you finally have a good idea." Benedito slapped him on the back.

Frank followed him out of the hardware store and down the street to a café where equally wizened men lounged around tables and eyed the surprisingly scantily clad local girls walking around. He didn't remember seeing quite so much exposed flesh in his last visits to the Azores and mentioned it to Ben.

The older man gave him an amused glance as he sipped his thick black coffee. "You sound like a cranky grandma. All they do is complain about the racy Brazilian soap operas influencing the girls nowadays, but the old ladies watch them all the same. Why not just enjoy the view?"

Frank shrugged. Girls half his age were children, not women. "Like I told you, I have Paulinha on my mind."

"Ah." He was uncharacteristically silent.

"What does *ah* mean?"

"Let me be blunt, Franco."

"How could I prevent it?" he murmured.

"Do not settle for a marriage without fire."

Well, he hadn't expected that. "What are you, a couples' counselor?"

"And how long have you been married, you young punk?" He took another sip. "You know I don't like to interfere…"

Frank almost snorted hot coffee out of his nose. "Since when?"

"Shut up and listen—this is serious. You would be miserable with her—not because she is not a nice woman, but because you are not in love with her."

"And how do you know?"

"Because you are fifteen hundred kilometers away on an island with an old man and not back on the mainland with her."

Frank made a dismissive gesture. "I have business here, not in Portugal."

"So you can't buy her a ticket to come with you? Are you too cheap or do you not want her here?"

He knew he was beat. "Love can come later."

"Or not at all."

"Enough about me. We have other errands to do." Benedito was one of his oldest friends and mentors, but he wasn't Frank's first choice for a romance advisor. Especially when what he said cut too close to the bone.

2

FASHIONISTA MAGAZINE IS thrilled to bring you *The Royal Review*—a hot new blog devoted to the upcoming wedding of Princess Stefania of Vinciguerra and her über-sexy, über-famous groom, Count Dieter von Thalberg, international soccer star. In less than two months, the stunning couple will say their "I do's" in the magnificent cathedral tucked away in the tiny, exclusive principality of Vinciguerra high in the Italian mountains.

Fashionista Magazine has an inside track with the royal lovebirds—last year, we brought you *Romance in Provence,* a blog written by American travel blogger Lily Adams about her trip to sunny, sensual Provence. Lily did more than write it, she *lived* it, and is now married to Princess Stefania's childhood friend, Count Jacques de Brissard, who owns the oldest lavender farm in the South of France. Countess Lily has kindly offered to fill us in on some of the inside scoop, with the bride's permission, of course!

One juicy detail—in a huge break from tradition, Princess Stefania will not have any bridesmaids—she'll have bridesmen! Her brother Giorgio, Lily's husband Jacques and their friend Francisco Duarte, Duke of Santas Aguas in Portugal, will be standing up with the bride.

"These men helped raise me after my parents passed away in their tragic car accident," said Stefania. "Along with my grandmother, they are the dearest people in the world to me. How could I not acknowledge that special relationship?"

Even the most jaded celebrity reporter has to admit to a certain misty eye at the tender sentiment. And the thought of those handsome men lined up in their formalwear is enough to make the heart go pitter-pat!

JULIA FOUND HERSELF wandering around the town again the next morning. Her parents had arrived safely in Boston and were on their way to the hospital to visit her aunt and uncle. She had rattled around the apartment for a few hours, cleaning things that didn't need cleaning until sheer boredom ran her out the door.

Boredom and a nagging curiosity about the man who looked so much like Frank. It could just be the familiar surroundings triggering her memory. The summer she and Frank had spent together had been magical, the summer after her first year in college. She attended Boston College but had gotten a cheap ticket to the Azores, a favorite place since her family had been stationed there for a year when she was a kid.

It was a favorite of Franco Duarte das Aguas Santas, especially since she'd found out later that his family owned their own small island there. He'd enjoyed America but was relieved to be home where he could speak Portuguese again after a few years in New York.

Julia heard plenty of Portuguese coming from the town square. She followed the noise and found a farmers' market full of fruits and vegetables, local honey and wine. The Azoreans didn't eat vegetables by themselves, either in a salad or cooked. The locals preferred to cook them into a soup filled with mostly meat, if they remembered the vegetables at all. She had discovered this after asking for a salad in the local restaurant and getting a blank stare. And when her neighbor had seen her eating a raw carrot as she sat in the garden, he told her those were either for the soup pot or the donkeys.

Julia had given a loud hee-haw, sending the man into a laughing fit that threatened to topple him.

But the fruit in the market was something more exciting. Baby bananas and golden-fleshed pineapples were on the table every morning. And her mother had made a great marmalade-type topping out of the local sour oranges, tart as lemons.

Julia picked up a packet of locally grown tea, the only tea grown in Europe, if she remembered correctly. And a jar of Azorean honey would sweeten it nicely. She paid a young lady for the tea and honey and wandered to a booth with Azorean wines and aperitifs. Too strong for her right now, although the bottles were beautiful. She declined a free sample but bought a bottle of the Aguardente velha da Graciosa brandy that her father liked and a bottle of passionfruit liqueur for her mother, who liked sweeter drinks.

A masculine laugh, full of joy and amusement rang in her ears. For a second, she thought she had fallen into the past again. But there it was again.

Not daring to breathe, she turned slowly, almost hoping she was just imagining it. She looked across the tables and saw him. The apple fell from her hand and clunked into the bin.

Frank stood across from her. She put her hand to her throat in shock. His raw masculinity at age twenty had matured into solid manhood, his shoulders broader, his arms thicker. His dark hair curled over his ears, one wave falling over his forehead. His face had hardened but his dark eyes crinkled with amusement.

Frank was leaning on a vegetable stand, listening to an older man who was obviously telling a funny story, thanks to the amused faces of the surrounding shoppers. Frank clapped the older man on the back and turned away, a smile on his face.

He saw her. The smile vanished, leaving a stunned expression to match hers. Instead of freezing, he moved. Toward her.

She panicked. What could she say to him? What would he say to her? She took a step backward, automatically searching for an escape.

But Frank was coming, cutting around the customers and tables with the grace she remembered. He stopped next to her. "Julia?" he asked, his voice full of disbelief. Good, so she wasn't the only one.

"Frank, well, my goodness! How in the world are you?" Her tone had enough sugar to frost a wedding cake. Light and friendly, light and friendly, she decided.

He didn't cooperate with her game plan and reply in an equally frothy manner, saying, *What brings you back to the Azores?* Or *Gee, Julia, how many years has it been?* Instead, he stood silently staring at her. Almost as if she were a ghost popping up through the floor.

"Frank?" She touched his forearm and he jumped as if she'd shocked him. She was shocked too and jerked her hand back.

Oh, no. Why that futile spark of attraction, after all these years? She looked away desperately.

"Julia. Your husband is here with you?" He casually scanned the crowd but his question was far from casual.

"My husband?" She wasn't thinking clearly, all the warning bells in her head distracting her, telling her to run away before she got hurt again. "No."

"No, he is not here, or no, you have no husband?"

"Oh, Franco," she whispered. He no longer fit his boyish nickname.

"Tell me, Julia. Which is it?"

"I have no husband."

Triumph flared in his eyes, quickly banked into a neutral expression. She resented it. As if she were a prize horse unexpectedly put up for auction.

"What about you? Any wife?" She meant it for turn-about, but he took it for interest, his mouth curling into a victorious smile.

Maybe it was interest. Oh, of course it was. She was dying to know if there was a Duchess Mrs. Franco Duarte, or whatever they were called in Portugal these days. She'd never quite picked up the naming system that could leave a person with four last names.

"No wife. Yet. I am here on business with Benedito." As if summoned by his name like Rumpelstiltskin, the wizened old man popped up at Frank's elbow.

"Bom dia, senhorina." He bowed at the waist, his

eyes sparkling with unabashed curiosity. Julia could well imagine why. She was probably pale as a ghost and Frank looked like the cat who'd swallowed the canary.

"Hello." Someone had to act with normalcy, so she extended her hand to the elderly Portuguese, who bowed over it almost as if she were a princess.

"Senhorina."

"Senhorina Julia Cooper, may I present *Senhor* Benedito Henriques Oliveira. Benedito, this is *Senhorina* Julia Cooper, whom I met here a long time ago."

The old man's eyes sharpened as he gazed between them. "A long time ago?"

"When we were younger," Frank answered evasively.

"Then you must talk!" Benedito practically shoved Frank at her. "Go to lunch! Don Franco, I will pick out those paint colors you wanted and have them mixed." He ducked away into the crowd as Frank let out a yelp of dismay.

"Paint colors?" Julia asked.

Frank gave up trying to spot his assistant and sighed. "We are here to fix up the villa."

"The villa." She was swept back in time again, to the stone building overlooking the sea on Frank's private island. "Why?" She immediately regretted showing any interest. It was his own business, even if he were setting it up for a bachelor pad.

"A honeymoon." He watched her closely.

"Ah." Of course Frank would have moved on. It wasn't as if he'd pined for her all these years. "And when is the happy event?"

"Two months, roughly. The wedding is in June."

Oh, the bitter irony. Over ten years since their separation and then she arrived two months before his wedding. "Well. May I congratulate you and the future duchess?"

He gave her a slow smile. "The wedding isn't mine."

FRANK DIDN'T FEEL THE slightest bit guilty about taking advantage of Julia's state of confusion to guide her into a cozy back table at a local café. She'd tried to hide her shock and then relief at finding out he wasn't the lucky groom, but Frank could still read her emotions, even after all these years.

"Would you like some wine?" He held the bottle over her glass, ready to pour. It was a variety they used to drink together.

She held up a hand. "Just water, please."

"All right." He ordered a bottle for her and filled her glass when it arrived. She drank eagerly, as if her throat were dry, then twirled the stem between her fingers. She looked all around the café—anywhere but at him.

"Julia," he began, not sure what to say. *Why did you leave me when we were college students?* sounded more than a bit whiny and pathetic. "How have you been?"

"Fine." She gave him a polite smile.

He tried again. "You finished your nursing degree?"

"Yes, and after a couple years, I went back to graduate school. I'm a nurse practitioner now and have taken some classes toward my doctoral degree."

"Good for you." Pride for her, misplaced or no, swelled his chest. "You always were the smartest woman I ever met."

The compliment broke through her polite shell and she snorted in disbelief. Now that was more like the old Julia he remembered. Or was it the young Julia he remembered? This woozy sense of past and present was mixing him up. "Why do you make that noise?"

"What?"

"You don't believe me." He shook his head. "Do you remember me as a liar?"

She pursed her lips. "Surely you've met smarter women than I."

"No, and just to prove it, all of them would have said 'smarter women than me.'"

"Good grammar doesn't make you smart."

He shook his head. "You always were terrible at accepting compliments." Like how her dark hair shone in the sun, her hazel eyes sparkling like his estate's premium sherry.

"I was not!"

"Argumentative, too."

"I am not—" She stopped arguing when he started to laugh. "Frank, that is not fair. You know I can't say anything to that without arguing."

"Then you'll just have to agree with me."

"Hmmph."

"Ah, Julia, no need to fuss. We are just old friends who have met again for lunch. What would you like to eat?"

She pressed her pretty pink lips together. Oh, how could he have forgotten how her dimples appeared when she did that. He had to hide a delighted smile before she really lost her temper and walked out on him. Again.

Well. Remembering *that* wiped the smile off his face.

"Frank?" She gave him a questioning look.

"Lunch, oh, yes."

"Where is the menu?"

He pointed to the chalkboard outside. "Whatever

they feel like cooking today. Chicken with rice, salt cod stew and *chouriço de carne*—sausage with fava beans."

"Mmm. I haven't had *chouriço* in years," she said wistfully.

"You can't get Portuguese sausage in Boston?" There was not only a huge Portuguese-American community there, but a large portion of that was specifically of Azorean heritage.

She shrugged. "I live in a different part of town."

That wasn't much of an answer. How long could it take her to drive to a Portuguese deli? He'd driven to Massachusetts and Rhode Island Portuguese restaurants from New York when he'd had a craving for sausage or the sweet, eggy desserts that were an Azorean specialty. "Well, you must have it here." He waved to the waiter and ordered the sausage and fava beans for her and the salt cod stew for him. "Sure you don't want any wine?"

She shook her head, so he ordered another bottle of water and switched to that, as well. Julia alone was making him light-headed enough.

He acknowledged she had become even more beautiful in the eleven years since they'd parted. "How is it that you aren't married yet?" he blurted, then winced. *Smooth move, dummy.* If she were married, she would either not be here at all or else her husband would be sitting across from him shooting daggers with his eyes at Frank. Maybe they'd have a few small kids, too, who would wonder in embarrassingly loud voices how this foreign guy used to know their mom.

"I'm not married yet because nobody ever asked me." Now her lips were really tight, her dimples even deeper.

"I did."

"Out of some misguided sense of obligation. That doesn't count."

He'd taken her virginity and changed her life forever—why wouldn't he feel obligated toward her? And it wasn't misguided, but he knew she would run away from him forever rather than discuss that now.

She jumped to her feet. "Look, Frank, it was nice to see you, but I have to go home."

He jumped up, too. "Julia, please stay. I spoke out of turn. I apologize." He shifted his body in front of her but the look of panic in her eyes made him move out of her way immediately. "But of course, I will not keep you here if you don't want to be." Frank wanted to kick himself. Good God, his prize bull at the estate had more finesse than he did.

She relaxed slightly, but was still wary, and he didn't blame her. The last time they'd parted, he'd been desperate to keep her and had been too overbearing. But twenty-year-old men in the agonies of first love were often thoughtless, and he'd been no exception. If he'd had a cooler head, he would have backed off, realizing the poor timing. Asking her to forgo the rest of her college education had been a bad idea, to put it mildly. "Come, sit. I promise, no more talk of awkward things. We will just be old friends who are catching up on the past ten years."

"Eleven," she corrected him automatically. So she remembered exactly, as well. That was intriguing.

"Eleven, of course." He took her elbow and guided her back to her seat. The waiter, sensing a juicy story, plied them with a basket full of hearty chunks of bread and fresh whipped butter. Frank practically had to shoo him away.

Julia seemed more amenable once she had a bit of homemade bread and butter in her, asking, "So who is getting married?"

Frank smiled. "Do you remember me telling you about my best friends from the university?"

She nodded. "The Italian guy and the French guy. Both were rich noblemen like you."

"Basically, yes. Giorgio—George—is the prince of Vinciguerra, a tiny country in the north of Italy. Jacques, who still goes by Jack, is a count, with his holdings in Provence, the south of France."

"And you, the Duke of Aguas Santas in Portugal."

"Yes." It wasn't any secret in the Azores who he was considering he owned a small island there. But the islanders were easygoing and not inclined to give him the paparazzi treatment. He was sure they gossiped about him, but friendly gossip was a national Portuguese pastime.

"Is one of them getting married?"

"Not exactly. Jack just got married last summer to an American travel writer named Lily, and Giorgio and his fiancée haven't set a date yet. It's for Giorgio's younger sister, Stefania, who lived with us in New York. She is marrying a German football star."

"Soccer." She lifted her chin. "Germans play soccer, not football."

He remembered Julia had been a star soccer player in high school and college. "No, football," he teased. "In Europe, we play football. And Stefania is getting married in the cathedral at home. Between the royal-watchers and the football fans, they will have very little privacy in their everyday lives, but Stefania and Dieter would like a private honeymoon. The villa is very private and romantic." At least that was how he'd remembered it when he and Julia had stayed there.

"Of course," she murmured, maybe remembering the same thing? "And that's why your assistant went off to pick paint colors."

Frank grimaced. "Benedito isn't exactly an interior designer. We'll have to see."

The waiter arrived with their entrees. Julia leaned over her bowl and eagerly inhaled the steam rising from the *chouriço*. She found a piece of the sausage with her fork and picked it up, waiting in anticipation before she moved it to her mouth. As she chewed, her expression was delighted and wistful in turns, as if she had been deprived of something important for so long, that the acquiring of it was almost bittersweet.

What else had Julia deprived herself of?

Frank watched her as long as he dared, then busied himself with his salt cod stew when she turned her attention back to him. *Bacalhoada,* or salt cod stew, was a Portuguese staple. The basics were the same everywhere, but it always tasted a bit different. Salt cod was dried and preserved with salt. To prepare it, you had to soak it overnight to rehydrate it, and then cook like any other fish. This dish was more of a casserole, with chunks of cod and *chouriço,* olive oil, potatoes and sliced tomatoes cooked along with them. Topping the dish were wedges of hardboiled eggs and black olives.

If Julia hadn't gone to any Portuguese places, it was unlikely she'd had *bacalhoada* either. He broke off a chunk of potato and salt cod with his fork, swirling it through the olive oil. "Here, try this." He offered her a taste, wondering if she'd accept.

She looked at him cautiously with her big sherry-colored eyes. He smiled as meekly as he could manage, when all he wanted to do was toss their bowls aside and drag her into his arms.

But none of that must have shown on his face because she delicately took the bite from his fork, chewing thoughtfully. "Um, very fishy."

He had to laugh. "Preserving the cod with salt concentrates its flavor."

"No, it's good. You know I like seafood."

"Yes, you do." They were both children of the ocean. She had made her mother's New England clam chowder for him once, and he had practically finished the stockpot in one sitting.

Julia ate steadily for a few minutes before speaking. "The villa doesn't need much work, does it? I mean, you probably use it several times a year."

"My mother and my sisters do. My nieces and nephews love fishing and exploring the island." Frank speared an egg wedge. Probably laid fresh this morning in the family henhouse.

"But you don't stay there."

"Once in a while." He'd tried to vacation there a few times, but seeing Julia's shadow in every room had made his visits short and far between. "There are a couple rooms that need to be painted, some garden work done and a thorough cleaning and airing. Oh, and I bought a beautiful new outdoor whirlpool tub that was just installed yesterday."

She smiled. "Sounds like a wonderful place for your friend's sister and her husband."

"Stefania is a real sweetheart. Hard to believe she's already twenty-four when I remember how little she was when she came to New York. Poor girl, losing both her parents at once." Stefania had been inconsolable. Her grandmother, fearing for her granddaughter's mental health, had sent Stefania to live with George, Jack and Frank. After hiring a housekeeper, the three nineteen-year-old guys raised Stefania through her preteen and teenage years. Frank shuddered at some of those memories.

"What was that shiver for?" Julia was eating heartily now, wiping her bowl with some bread. He was glad to see that since she looked a bit thin.

"Stefania always has been a handful. She once chained herself and her electronic bullhorn to a lamppost outside a certain foreign consulate whose country was not particularly kind to its women and children."

Julia burst out laughing.

"She called every media outlet in New York, drew a crowd of several hundred enthusiastic supporters and wound up on the national nightly news. When one reporter tried to take her to task for being the product of an outdated patriarchal monarchy, she told her how her own country had granted women the vote twenty years before America and how her outdated patriarchal monarchy had a female literacy rate of one hundred percent compared to that consulate's country's dismal rate of fourteen percent."

"Good for Stefania. Blasted them with facts. And what does she do now?"

"She's finishing her master's degree in international politics and will probably stay in New York since

George is running their own country very well. She'd
let him know if he weren't."

"You have to keep politicians on their toes."

"She also will be selling a commemorative perfume
made from lavender at Jack's French estate. Proceeds
go to her women's and children's charity."

"What an accomplished young woman. Give her my
best wishes if you get the chance." Julia sipped her water
and pushed her bowl away. "That is so filling. I can't
believe I ate all of that."

"Our food is comfort food. Nothing low carb or low
fat about it." Frank finished his own helping. "And now
for dessert."

"No, Frank," she groaned. "I may pop."

He didn't want her to go yet, but forcefeeding her
was probably not the way to spend more time with her.
Maybe bribing her with food? "How about we take a
couple pastries with us? We can go for a walk, pick up
some coffee and then you can try one."

She hesitated. "Okay. That way I don't have to cook
dinner for myself."

He signaled the waiter to order before she changed
her mind. The waiter brought him a box of pastries
and Frank paid the tab, despite Julia's protest that she
wanted to pitch in. Frank and the waiter gave her such
an incredulous glance that she subsided.

Frank hid a smile. He may have been educated in
the United States, a more modern version of his ducal
ancestors, but there was no way in hell a woman would
pay for her own meal on a date with him.

And whether Julia realized it or not, liked it or not,
it *was* a date.

3

JULIA FOUGHT THE BUTTERFLIES in her stomach as she walked next to Frank. Their lunch had felt suspiciously like a date—not that she and Frank had bothered to date very long the first time they'd met.

Her teenage self had wanted to blow off steam after her first stressful year in college, and sexy Frank had been more than willing to help. But it had quickly turned to more.

She sneaked a look at his profile. He'd lost his eager openness of earlier years, but what did she expect? She wasn't exactly a fresh-faced innocent any longer, either.

Frank caught her looking at him. She thought he'd make something of that, but all he asked was how she'd decided to come to the Azores again.

She chewed her lip for a second and decided to tell him a partial truth. "I was hurt at work and needed to take some time off to recover."

"What?" He stopped in his tracks. "But you should be at home resting." He took her hand and tucked it into the bend of his elbow.

She automatically tightened her grip on his bicep. "You're stronger than you used to be."

He covered her hand with his. "I work with the men on the estate back home. We still have the big vineyard, several orchards, and we raise cattle, horses and sheep. After college in New York, I apprenticed myself to Benedito and learned as many of the jobs as I could."

"Which is your favorite part?"

He gave her a startled look, as if he'd never considered that. "My favorite part is making sure my people have steady jobs and can provide for their families." He smiled down at her. "Although I admit I like working with the bulls. Matching my strength and wits against them keeps me on my toes."

Frank had always reminded her of a bull—strong, stubborn and sexually insatiable. Memories of his stamina and endurance made her catch her breath and stumble on a loose cobblestone. He steadied her instantly, his arm flexing. "Are you all right?"

"Fine, just the uneven street." And she was tiring. The emotional expense of meeting Frank again and trying to stay on guard with him during lunch had sapped her strength. And thinking about how they'd spent the majority of their time together having the hottest sex of her life was not exactly keeping her mind on difficult things. Like walking.

Did he remember much about their summer together? He was a rich, famous nobleman, so undoubtedly he'd had plenty of hot sex since then. Probably had women throwing themselves at him every other week. Supermodels, princesses, gold-diggers…and probably very nice ladies who would be thrilled to marry a handsome, sexy man like Franco Duarte das Aguas Santas.

"Come on, Julia." For a second she thought he was reading her mind. "Let's go sit in the park." He deposited her at a bench and disappeared into a nearby café, returning with two paper cups of coffee. "Two creams, two sugars." He handed her one.

At her surprised look, he stopped. "Or do you drink it differently now?"

"No, that's just fine." On her night shifts in the E.R., she'd been teased for putting so much cream and sweetener in her coffee. "And you still drink it black?"

"Of course. It is a sign of extreme manliness." He laughed and opened the pastry box. "Here are some *pastéis de nata.*"

"Oh, my," she whispered. "I haven't had one in…"

"Eleven years?" he asked, raising his eyebrows.

"Yes." She stared at the small round egg custard tarts, almost afraid to take a bite. Why had she ever thought coming back to the Azores was a good idea? These tarts were the apple in her Garden of Eden.

Frank closed the box, and she looked into his sad eyes. "Was it really so terrible, Julia?"

"What?" she asked, startled. How did he know about her accident in the hospital? Not an accident, she mentally corrected herself. It hadn't been an accident.

"You loved Portuguese food and cooked it every day for us, but you haven't touched it since we parted, did you? Did our time together give you such terrible memories?"

"Never!" she blurted and then sipped her coffee to look away from him.

He didn't say anything, only opened the pastry box again. "Open your mouth, my sweet Julia."

She did open her mouth, but only to tell him she

wasn't his sweet Julia anymore, but he took advantage of it to brush a tart across her lips.

A flaky crumb stuck to her bottom lip and she automatically licked it off.

He inhaled sharply. "That's it. Now take a bite."

She clamped her mouth tight and he had the nerve to laugh. "Oh, Julia, you wish to see which one of us is more stubborn? Or are you afraid of a little sweetness?"

She snorted in derision. He pulled the tart away from her and bit into it with his straight white teeth that had never required fillings or braces, she remembered. "Mmm. Oh, so good. Imagine how good it would be after such a long, dry spell."

Julia had the sneaking suspicion they weren't discussing tarts anymore. Unless it was her. Hell, she was feeling like a tart now, watching his strong lips nibbling at the crispy pastry crust. He darted his tongue out to lick the soft, creamy egg filling and she wanted those lips, that tongue, to devour her with the same intensity. He finished the pastry and she almost groaned with disappointment. After feeling half-alive for so long, the rush of desire hurt, as if she'd fallen asleep on her arm and had to endure its pins-and-needles reawakening. Much more painful when it was your entire mind and body.

"Come on, Julia." He held another out to her, daring her to take it.

She did and cautiously bit into it. Sugar, cinnamon and cream burst on her tongue and she actually moaned. Frank's fingers dented the corners of the box at the blatantly sexual sound. She finished it quickly and reached into the box for another.

"Not so fast, greedy girl." He pulled the box away and got out a tart. "If you want another, I'll give it to you."

Her nipples tightened and she knew they had passed the point of friendly lunches. The point of no return was rushing up rapidly, and she didn't want to stop. "What are you waiting for?" she challenged.

"To see if you were ready."

"I am." She glared at him and opened her mouth.

He laughed. "You look like you're at the dentist. Relax."

Julia forced herself to breathe. He held the pastry to her lips, making her take the next step. She nibbled at the crust, and he scoffed. "You used to be so much braver than this. What happened?"

He had no idea what had happened to her. She opened her mouth wide and snapped down on the tart, barely missing his fingers. "That better?" she asked, once she had finished chewing.

Frank tossed the tart box to the side. "Finally a sign of passion." He dragged her into his arms. She expected him to kiss her right away, but instead he looked down into her face. "Julia." It was full of wonder and tenderness. "After all these years."

"It shouldn't be any longer." She wrapped her arms around his neck and pulled his mouth to hers. They moaned simultaneously as their lips met.

She wanted to weep, to sing, to dance around the park. Here he was, and he was kissing her, the pent-up passion bursting free from both of them.

His mouth was soft and warm as he explored the contours of hers. He pressed kisses along the seam of her lips, nibbling at her full bottom lip.

She sighed in pleasure and opened to his further exploration. He flicked his tongue inside to meet hers, tasting of sweet pastry and coffee. She ran her tongue along his and pressed closer to him. His hands tightened on her shoulders and he groaned deep in his throat.

Julia's head spun, as if she had been living in a gray world and it suddenly turned into color. As if she had only eaten watery oatmeal for years and was offered a banquet instead. Frank was a feast for her senses, wine for her thirst.

He brushed her hair aside and trailed kisses down her neck. How did he remember what she liked? She ran her fingers through his thick black hair, enjoying how it fell into waves under her touch. Heat poured off him, engulfing her in quiet flame.

Their silent solace was interrupted by the angry buzzing of an engine. She dragged her eyes open to see a wide-eyed park gardener butchering the grass in wobbly stripes thanks to his inattentiveness.

"Frank." She pushed at his shoulders but may as well have been pushing at the park's statue for all the good it did. He fastened his mouth on the hollow below her ear and sucked, causing her to nearly see stars. Good Lord, if only he could do that elsewhere…

But she also knew how much he would dislike being the focus of gossip. "Frank, we have company." She tried shoving him again and this time he raised his head.

His olive skin was flushed with desire, his eyes black with lust, hypnotizing her as if he were a dangerous lion and she were his prey. He could devour her anytime.

He shook his head as if coming back to himself and glared at the nosy gardener. The young man immediately turned back to his work and Frank's mouth tightened. "Come with me." He stood and took her hand in his.

They ducked out of sight down a small pathway. He stopped under a tree. "Julia, I want to see you again."

She crazily considered inviting him home, or rather to her parents' apartment. Ugh. Not that. "When?"

"As soon as possible. I have to take our supplies back to Belas Aguas, but it is only a half hour by boat." Belas Aguas, Beautiful Waters, was his family's private island, in their possession for hundreds of years.

A faint ache was starting in the side of her head, a warning to get home and lie down before it grew. "Tomorrow." She didn't want to discuss her injury yet, and she was already overwhelmed.

"Tomorrow." He looked disappointed but kissed her gently. "You have a phone here?"

They exchanged numbers, Julia's fingers fumbling over the keypad as she entered his. "Frank…" She stared up at him, her headache tightening.

"You look pale again." He tucked her hand in his elbow. "I'll take you home so you can rest. I'll pick you up at one tomorrow. We can have lunch at the villa if you're up for a boat ride."

"I'll be fine." She waved her free hand.

"Good." He guided her out of the park and through the streets, chatting to her about the plans for Stefania's wedding. "The wedding is in June at the big cathedral in their country of Vinciguerra. I've been helping Stefania with some things, like choosing colors, invitations and flowers. It's amazing what you can do with webcam conferencing. And it helps to have their country's department of protocol doing the heavy lifting." He laughed. "My mother told me I had no idea how much work went into planning a high-society wedding, much less a royal wedding. She was right. But everything is just what Stefania wants, so that's all that matters."

Julia smiled. Frank, macho nobleman and rancher, had thrown himself into wedding preparations. She wondered if he had ever come close to planning a wedding for himself. Maybe she'd break her self-imposed rule and look him up on the internet. She never had before, somehow knowing keeping tabs on him would only make their separation worse.

She pointed out the turn to her parents' street and they climbed the small hill to the old farmhouse. Working in his garden, *Senhor* de Sousa eyed them with avid curiosity as they passed. Frank called out a greeting, and her neighbor bobbed his head respectfully, obviously knowing who Frank was.

Frank guided her up the steps and into the small living room. She was acutely aware of her bedroom right around the corner, but the only thing she wanted to do was lie down—alone.

"I should leave right away." Frank smiled down at her. "Your reputation is on the line."

"Hmmph." She wasn't used to considering the state of her virtue, but small-town gossip about her would reflect poorly on her mother and dad.

"But I do have time for this." He leaned forward and pressed a soft kiss on her mouth. She caught his shoulders and pulled him close. His lips moved over hers gently, then more demanding. She moved in close to him, intoxicated by his clean scent, his hot masculinity. She opened her mouth to him and he slid his tongue inside to caress hers. Her arms curved around his neck and he backed her against the small couch. She almost lost her balance and he steadied her.

Once he was sure she had her balance, he groaned and moved away. "Julia, you tempt me terribly. I am putty in your hands."

She'd bet he'd be a lot firmer than that. But she managed to back away, putting the table between them. "My parents..." she gestured.

"Of course. This is their home." He rubbed his face. "One o'clock tomorrow. We can have lunch on the terrace at the villa. I'll send Benedito to the far side of the island and have him cut weeds or something."

"Frank!" she scolded. "He seems perfectly nice."

He rolled his eyes. "Don't let his cheerful elfin looks fool you. He's a thorn in my side."

"But he's your right hand."

"That, too." Frank smiled at her. "Enough about Benedito. Tomorrow is for us."

"Okay." Her voice suddenly sounded breathy and seductive. He noticed that as well, running his gaze down her body.

"Tomorrow." He took a deep breath, repeating her words as if he were promising himself—and her—a treat. "Lock the door behind me." He winked and left.

Julia blew out a long breath. She had the sneaking suspicion that she would have asked him to stay, parents' home or no, if her head had been feeling better.

She went into the kitchen and took a pain pill with some fresh juice before lying down in her lonely bed. She pulled a quilt over herself, but it was no substitute for a warm male body. Was it a good idea to invite Frank to share her bed? She just couldn't decide. Her mind was telling her no but her body, well, it had a mind of its own.

4

BENEDITO HAD BEEN uncharacteristically quiet on the boat ride back to Frank's family's island. The two men carried several boxes of food and building supplies into the villa.

Frank set a bag of bread, meat and cheese on the large oak worktable in the center of the kitchen.

Benedito set a couple bottles of red wine next to it. "I will get more wine tomorrow, but this should be enough for tonight."

Frank nodded, but he wasn't about to drink a whole bottle on his own and show up hungover to pick up Julia. Benedito had an inordinate capacity for *vinho* and would not show a single bad after-effect.

The kitchen was bigger than most in the Azores, the stove and oven wall tiled in blue-and-red Portuguese tiles and inset oak cabinets. The exposed walls had been sponge-painted peach and gold over beige in some unfortunate past decade and Frank was planning to change that. The master bathroom was powder pink, his mother's favorite color, but probably not Stefania's, the bride-to-be's.

On the other hand, Stefania and her groom probably didn't give a fig about the wall color and only wanted a big soft bed. That certainly had been his first priority when he and Julia had stayed there.

Unfortunately they had leapt before they looked, straight into bed. He didn't ever regret making love with her, but in the end, it hadn't been enough to keep them together. What a miracle that had brought them both back to the Azores at the same time.

Somehow the uncanny Benedito had read his mind. "Don Franco, did you have a nice lunch with the *senhorina?*"

"How did you know I had lunch with her?" He made cheese and sausage sandwiches on crusty bread for him and Benedito and put the rest of the food away.

"The waiter is my second cousin's daughter-in-law's brother." Benedito opened one bottle of wine and a plastic container of marinated olives from the farmers' market. He poured the wine and ate the olives out of the container with his gnarled fingers. Benedito abandoned his manners with gusto when he was away from his wife.

He offered some to Frank, who gave up on his own manners and accepted. Pure heaven. "A close family connection," he said sardonically. "Yes, we had a nice lunch and then had coffee and *pastéis de nata* in the park." He'd left the box with Julia—she looked as if she could stand to gain some weight.

"Ah, yes, the park." Benedito nodded knowingly. "Quite the box of *pastéis* it was." He made a zipping motion across his lips and winked.

"How do you know that? Were you skulking in the shrubbery or is the gardener there your nephew?" He restrained himself from chucking an olive—or the entire container—at Benedito's head.

"Leonor's nephew."

"Of course." Frank sighed. A fishbowl of a life, that's what he led. And of course, Benedito had ducked the question if he had indeed been skulking in the shrubbery. It was fair to say Frank wouldn't have noticed if the entire Portuguese Army had been doing reconnaissance missions in the bushes. He finished his sandwich and turned on his laptop to do some business. "Benedito, can you install the new faucet in the downstairs powder room? The old one is leaking." If Benedito was busy, maybe he would stop bugging Frank.

No such luck. "*Senhorina* Julia certainly is beautiful."

"Mmm-hmm." Frank stared at his email program, mentally willing him to go away. Two dozen emails from various people on his estates.

"She is very smart, an advanced nurse in a big American hospital, according to her neighbors."

"Yes." Good Lord, the old man had been busy this afternoon.

"A wonderful companion for any red-blooded man."

That was hovering on the border of disrespect, even if Frank knew exactly what he was talking about and agreed one hundred percent. He lifted his eyebrow and scowled at Benedito.

"Will you be seeing the *senhorina* again?" the old man pressed.

"Maybe if I can get some privacy for once!" Frank shouted, finally losing his temper. "With waiters and gardeners and neighbors all reporting back to you as if you were my guardian and I were a virginal princess out in the world for the first time? How do you expect me to do anything with her? Tell me that!"

"Ah, to be alone." Benedito nodded, his eyes wide, as if the idea of privacy was a new and strange concept. To him, of course, it was. "Don Franco, if you would excuse me, I have to check on some building supplies."

"Fine, go." Frank waved his hand and forced himself to read his email from the mainland. Problems with wine caskets, grapevines, animals needing the vet, two of his fieldhands fighting over the same girl. Fortunately, relatively small things, although Frank recalled the girl in question being quite pretty and flirtatious. And with a mean, burly father. He toyed with the idea of inquiring whether the two fieldhands had turned up with black eyes and fat lips received *after* their fight, but the more he stayed out of their personal business, the more smoothly it ran.

Involving the Duke in romantic quarrels would bring shame and embarrassment upon the parties involved. Better that the Duke focused on his own romantic problems. And even better that the Duke stopped referring to himself in the third person.

Frank grinned and immersed himself in estate business for the next couple hours, thoughts of Julia always at the edges of his mind.

Benedito popped into the kitchen again. "*Boa tarde,* Don Franco."

"Yes, good evening to you, too. Did you take care of those building supplies?"

"Yes, and picked up the paint, as well."

"Paint? But we never chose any colors."

"But I did, Don Franco. So you would have more

time to spend with the young lady." Benedito nodded conspiratorially.

Frank bit back a groan and thanked him. What hideous palette did Benedito choose?

"And Don Franco, I received a call from the mainland."

"You did?" He didn't even know Benedito had a cell phone.

"Yes, yes." Benedito waved his hands impatiently. "Leonor, my beloved wife…" He paused dramatically.

"Yes, I know who she is." Leonor was the housekeeper at the *fazenda*. In addition to the traditional agricultural holdings for an annual pittance Frank leased use of several outbuildings for small local businesses and artists' studios. It boosted local income and kept families together since they didn't have to send the men and young people off to Lisbon for jobs.

"Leonor needs me at home."

"Is she all right?" Frank asked. Leonor had the constitution of a mule and if local legend was correct, had last been ill in the early 1980s—a mild cold.

"She, ah…she, well…she has, um, female problems!" Benedito finished triumphantly.

Frank supposed it was possible, not being in that line of work, although Leonor had to be in her late sixties. But the magical phrase "female problems" was like playing the ace in a game of poker—the trump card that nobody argued with. "Female problems."

"Yes, yes. Oh, terrible female problems." Benedito shuddered at the horror, whether real or imagined.

"And I suppose they came on suddenly and you need to rush back to the *fazenda* to help care for her."

"Oh, Don Franco, I am glad you understand."

Frank clapped him on the back. "I do indeed. When do we leave?"

"We?" Benedito's dismay was comical. "No, no, Don Franco, it would be a sin, a sin, I tell you, if my poor little problems were to take you away from your business here in the islands." He drew himself up. "I will call my wife and tell her—" he paused for effect "—that you need me here. She will manage." He looked nobly across the sea toward the mainland, the brave husband separated from his ailing wife.

Oh, bravo. Frank was ninety-nine percent convinced Benedito was lying through his coffee-stained teeth, but what if Leonor were indeed ill?

"Oh, go on. Go home." He waved his hand at Benedito.

"Thank you, Your Grace." Benedito clutched his hand, but when he bent to kiss it, Frank had enough.

"No more of the grateful peasant routine! Why aren't you more agreeable to me the rest of the time?"

Benedito widened his eyes. "Your Grace, I have no idea what you mean."

Frank decided to see if Benedito actually had a phone or was lying even more. "Call the blasted airline and change your return flight."

His eyes darted back and forth. "My phone, the battery failed just as I was saying goodbye to my dear wife. It stopped right in the middle of hearing her precious voice, right in the middle of our tender farewells…"

Frank tossed him his phone, cutting off the rest of his nauseating description. "Here, use this."

"Yes, Your Grace," Benedito said meekly, turning his back to make his call.

"Peasants," Frank grumbled. "Everything went to hell when we were no longer allowed to whip them."

The older man's shoulders stiffened in outrage and Frank grinned. Served him right, although he had his doubts about being able to best Benedito in a physical fight. The wily old man undoubtedly fought dirty. Still, Frank was glad to get in the last word. For once.

"Your faucet is installed, Your Grace," Benedito announced in long-suffering tones, coming up behind Frank as he waded through a dreary email announcement of new rules from the ministry of agriculture. "I skinned my knuckles on the old sink and I think they are infected."

Frank rolled his eyes. "Too soon for infection. Let me see." He gestured to Benedito to extend his hand for inspection.

"Eh, what do you know about injuries?" Benedito clutched his hand to his chest. "Maybe I should go to São Miguel."

"The hospital? If you're seriously injured, I'll take you over there myself."

"Pah, the hospital!" Benedito spat. "Full of germs and sick people."

"Well, yes. They do have both of those."

"I was thinking that pretty nurse could look at my wounds."

"Julia?"

"Yes, *Senhorina* Julia, with the beautiful black hair." Benedito sounded half in love with her already.

Frank beat down a weird jealous twinge. For goodness' sake, Benedito was old enough to be her father. "Oh, let me see this mangled hand of yours."

After a brief tussle where Benedito refused to show Frank his hand, Frank finally got it yanked away and looked. "Those three scrapes? Your wife would fall on the ground laughing if you asked her to take you to the hospital for that."

He jerked his arm away. "My wife is not here. She is ailing, poor woman, and I am alone on this island with an unsympathetic duke who mocks my injury."

"How about some disinfectant spray and bandages? Besides, you're flying home to the mainland, when?"

"Tomorrow."

"Maybe when you take your wife to the doctor for her 'female problems,' they can look at your hand."

Benedito pursed his lips. "If Your Grace refuses…"

"I'm not taking you to see Julia for skinned knuckles. Do you know how hard I had to work to get her to go to lunch with me? And she's coming to the island for the afternoon tomorrow as soon as I drop you at the airport."

"Well, why didn't you say so?" Benedito beamed at him as if he were a particularly stupid student who had finally done something smart. Whistling a ribald folktune, he strutted over to the sink and scrubbed his fingers without even wincing.

"Why, you old faker!" Frank didn't know whether to throw something at him or give him a raise. "You were looking for an excuse to get me to see her again?"

His only reply was an innocent shrug. "I feel much better already. Perhaps it is your healing presence."

"I'm a duke, not a saint. Now, don't you have some packing to do?"

"I have plenty of work to do before I leave, Don

Franco. But continue your own work. You will not hear a peep from old Benedito."

That was what worried him. Like his sisters' kids, Benedito was only quiet when looking for trouble.

He shook his head as Benedito scooted out of the kitchen. Frank's phone rang and he answered. "George?"

"Frank, glad I caught you." It was his best friend from college and brother of the bride. George's relaxed voice came over the satellite connection. Of course he always sounded relaxed, being in love with Renata, his beautiful and sexy American fiancée. "How have you been?"

"Keeping busy with getting the villa in order. It just needs some cosmetic work and a bit of cleaning."

"Oh, so you're in the Azores? I was wondering why the connection took a little while longer. How is it?"

"Lovely as ever."

"What? You hate being out there anymore. The last couple times you barely stayed long enough to get your luggage off the boat."

Frank grinned. "Let's just say things are coming full circle."

"What? I better call Jack. You sound like you've taken too much cold medication."

"George..." He rolled his eyes but greeted Jack dutifully. George and Frank had been his best men at Jack's whirlwind wedding in Philadelphia last summer. George had met Lily, Jack's beautiful American bride, and they had all gone out for cheesesteaks and fries. Yum.

"Frank's in the Azores," George announced. "And he's enjoying himself."

"That's great. Congratulate me, *mes amis!*" Jack cried. "I wasn't going to say anything, but I can't wait to announce to you, my brothers—Lily and I are having a baby."

A stunned hush fell over the group.

"A baby," Frank finally choked out, fighting back bittersweet memories. "Jack, that's wonderful."

"Amazing." George's voice sounded husky, as well. "And how is your lovely wife feeling?"

"Ah, not so good." He lowered his voice. "I tried to tell her that illness is a good sign that the hormones are strong and working well, but all she did was call me bad names. In French, no less. She picked it up from the farm workers—I'll have to take my manager to task for allowing such vulgarity." But he sounded giddy and not about to punish anybody.

"Renata and I are going to have a baby," George announced.

"What?" they chorused.

"No, not now. As soon as Renata and I are married. I cannot have the next Prince of Vinciguerra born less than nine months after our wedding. Just my luck he would be a ten-pound baby and nobody would believe he was early."

Frank nodded. "Don't want any doubt about succession to the throne."

"Exactly," George agreed. "But enough about babies—at least for now, Jack. Do keep us posted."

"But of course. How is your lovely island, Frank?"

"About to get lovelier at one o'clock tomorrow." He took a deep breath. "I don't know if you remember, but many, many years ago, I stayed the summer here."

"Yes?" they answered cautiously, remembering the

terrible autumn that had followed when Frank had become a mess, a zombie unable to function without Julia.

"I don't know if it is fate or luck, but I am here—and so is she."

"She? You mean Julia?" George knew that name well, having listened to Frank cry in his beer for weeks.

"But how can that be? Did you find her and invite her?" Jack sounded confused.

"Her parents live here now and she was visiting them. They are back in the States with elderly relatives, and I have her all to myself."

"Oh." George paused for a couple seconds. "And how is Julia?" he asked politely.

"Single and more beautiful than ever."

"Please, Frank, just be careful," Jack urged him. "People do change after all these years. You are different. She will be different. You cannot expect to pick up where you left off."

"Why would I want to do that? We left off with her leaving me, Jack." Frank was getting irritated. His best friends had found the loves of their lives, and Jack was having a baby, as well.

"I think Jack is just concerned for you, Frank," George added, ever the diplomat. "Obviously you are a grown man now, with more experience in matters of the heart. But sometimes you see things with rose-colored glasses, as the American phrase goes. Take a good look at the situation with as much clarity as you can."

"Like you two did with Renata and Lily?" he asked pointedly.

There was silence and then two voices breaking into

guilty laughter. "Do as we say, not as we do, Frank," Jack said.

"Ah, yes, we did not listen to our own advice, did we, Jack?"

"Not at all. But it all turned out well in the end."

"And maybe it will for me and Julia, too."

"If that is your wish, we certainly hope so," Jack said.

"I don't know," Frank said thoughtfully. "I was a wreck when she left me the first time. Should I risk it?"

George sighed. "Life is full of risk." His own parents had not lived past their mid-forties. "All we can do is live for the moment and hope for the best."

"Very true. Fate can be cruel," Jack agreed, having seen plenty of tragedies as a disaster-relief physician. Frank didn't even want to imagine what he had witnessed over his years of work.

Frank congratulated Jack on his baby-to-be and wrote down some important wedding dates from George before hanging up. He had just enough time to finish at the villa before he needed to check in at the estates and then go to the wedding in Vinciguerra.

But as he worked on more estate business, he thought about what George and Jack had said about the vagaries of fate.

Frank didn't want any risk. He was a farmer and rancher. Uncertainty was dangerous. The seasons turned, the crops were planted and harvested, animals were born and grew. The Dukes of Aguas Santas were born and grew. And died, like his own father twenty years before.

But Frank was the last and only Duke. Without him, there were only his sisters, who were uninterested and unprepared to run the estate. And to maintain everything until their children were old enough? Almost impossible. Without proper management, his estates would decline and be sold, the title of Duke of Aguas Santas a title in name only for his oldest nephew.

He drummed his fingers on the table. Until meeting Julia again, he had planned to court his sister's friend, Paulinha. Now that plan was on the scrap heap. Julia was the only woman who made him feel, made him alive. But as his friends had so unwelcomely pointed out, people changed. Maybe he and Julia had changed enough that they could stay together this time.

5

Fashionista Magazine: The Royal Review:

UNTIL NOW, PRINCESS Stefania has been hush-hush over many of the fashion details of her big day, but she finally told our loyal royal correspondent Countess Lily de Brissard how she's decided to wear her hair. Long and loose or fabulous up-do? A little of both, it turns out. "I have a small face and lots of curly hair," explained Princess Stefania. "So I plan to pull the top and sides back in a smooth do, while letting the back hang loose and curly. This way, I can have my hair out of my face but still have my natural look."

Princess Stefania also has something very special for the "something old" category of the old wedding rhyme—"Something old, something new, something borrowed, something blue." "I will be wearing my grandmother's own bridal veil from her wedding more than fifty years ago. It was handmade in Belgium and is the finest, most delicate lace imaginable. They don't make lace like that anymore, and I'm so proud to wear it in my grandmother's honor."

JULIA PACED THE STONE FLOOR in the apartment's living room. As she passed the mirror over the small table, she caught sight of her hair and stopped to examine it.

What had she been thinking to get a haircut this morning? She had been walking by the small beauty salon and had impulsively gone in to see what they could do with her mop of hair.

Despite her borderline Portuguese language skills, she hadn't accidentally told them to give her a crew cut or Mohawk. Although the ladies had tsked over the sad condition of her hair, they had done yeoman's work to get rid of the frizzy ends and coax it into big ringlets to air dry. Since she'd always pulled her hair back into a headband or ponytail, she'd never bothered having a "day-off" hairstyle.

She tossed her head and let the curls bounce against her cheeks. The hairstylists had also done her makeup for her when she told them she had a lunch date. She looked better than she had in months. Years, more like, she told herself wryly. Graduate school and overnights in the E.R. hadn't exactly put a bloom in her cheeks.

She turned away from the mirror and spied the clock. Frank was coming in just a few minutes. What was she supposed to bring for an afternoon on the island? A jacket, sunglasses and sunblock were easy choices. But what else? She looked down at her denim capri pants and short-sleeved coral-colored blouse with small ruffles framing the button-down center. She had strapped on black patent wedge sandals that showed off her new coral pedicure.

A knock sounded at the wooden door, and she spun toward it, then back to the mirror, then back to the door. She forced her breathing to slow and pasted a bright smile on her face, determined not to show any nerves.

Julia opened the door and greeted Frank with what she hoped was a good mix of casual friendliness. "Hello! How are you? How was the boat ride?"

Frank ignored her outstretched hand and swept her into his arms. His mouth carelessly destroyed her peach lip gloss and her hard-fought nonchalance. She quickly surrendered and eagerly clung to him, enjoying the stroke of his tongue and the pressure of his hands on her waist, his strong fingers straying deliciously close to her bottom.

He finally lifted his head. "Hello to you, too, I'm much better now that I've seen you and the boat ride was just fine."

"Oh. Good." She made herself ease away and checked her lipgloss in the mirror.

He came up behind her, his black hair touching hers in their reflection, just a shade darker than her dark brown. "I like your curls." He wrapped one around his fingers and brought it to his face. "You smell like ripe, juicy peaches." His expression made it clear that he liked peaches.

"Glad you like it," she stammered. "It's been a while since I had a trim."

He theatrically patted his own hair. "Me, too." He seemed to sense her nervousness and stepped away. "I'll have to get a haircut before Stefania's wedding. She told me I was getting shaggy the last time we web-conferenced."

"Lots to do before a wedding. My brother's wedding

seemed more complicated than the invasion of Normandy, and I thought the mother of the bride was going to have a nervous breakdown before it was over. My own mother wasn't far behind."

"Oh, yes, I remember my sisters' weddings. Fortunately I was in school for much of the preparation." He looked around the living room. "Do you have a jacket? The wind can be cool on the water."

She reached for a spring-green windbreaker and her tan leather handbag and locked the door behind them. Fortunately *Senhor* de Sousa was nowhere in sight but was probably peering out past the curtains. They walked down the hill through the town and to the docks, Frank tucking her hand into his arm as they walked.

"Watch your step," he cautioned as they arrived at the docks. He guided her over the boards to a large launch for a rather small yacht. She was no naval expert, having a better eye for airplanes, but it looked to be perfectly adequate for traveling the fifteen or so miles to Belas Aguas.

The boat was locked up tight with no sight of Frank's assistant. "What project is your friend Benedito working on?"

"Hopefully catching his flight back to Lisbon." Frank stepped onto the boat first and helped her aboard.

"What?" They were alone? All alone?

"No, I didn't try to get rid of him." Frank smiled at her. "He said his wife had called with a medical issue and he needed to get back to the *fazenda* to care for her. I'm going to start the boat." He climbed the short flight of stairs to the enclosed bridge and unlocked the door.

Julia's antennae popped up and she followed him.

Diagnosis had always been one of the favorite parts of her job. "What kind of medical issue?"

He turned over the engine, which came to life with a dignified roar. "Ah, that intrigues you." He raised his voice to be heard over the engine. "However, I'm unable to provide any more information except that they were 'female problems.'"

"That could cover a lot of different things." And many women were understandably reluctant to discuss gynecological problems with men, especially a husband's boss.

"Leonor has always been very healthy so I am sure everything will be all right." He smiled at her and then went back to checking various gauges and dials on the control panel.

"It's good of you to let him go back considering all the work you have left."

He gave her an amused look tinged with exasperation. "We're not in the business of oppressing peasants anymore, Julia. The man tells me his wife is sick, he goes to her. He's not a serf."

"Of course." She'd never gotten used to the idea that he was literally the lord of the manor and assumed some old rules still applied.

"Make yourself comfortable while I untie the boat." Frank flicked one of her curls as he passed her, and a warm feeling banished some of the anxiety in her stomach.

She peered out the back window at the deck. The boat had room for several sunbathers and she guessed there was probably a good-size galley, or kitchen, in the level below the bridge.

Frank worked easily, undoing the lines and making

sure the boat was clear. He stopped to greet a passing deckhand, who quickly lost his awe of the Duke of Santas Aguas after a minute of masculine banter. Julia could only imagine what joke caused the two of them to break into laughter.

The deckhand was still grinning as he strolled away and Frank whistled a tune as he disappeared from sight to the front of the boat.

Julia looked out to sea. Looked like clear sailing, or motoring rather. She heard Frank's steps. "A nice day to be on the water."

He grinned. "For the forty or so minutes we'll be on it."

"The clouds are beautiful—bright white and puffy." She laughed. "My dad would kill me if he heard me describing them that way. Being in the Air Force, he was a meteorology expert and made me call them by the proper names."

Frank checked the dials once more and then hit a button that started a grinding noise. "That's to lift the anchor," he explained. "What kind of clouds do we have today in the beautiful Azores?"

"Since the Azores are almost four hundred miles from end to end, I can't presume to speak for the rest of the islands."

He nodded his head gravely but she could see the twinkle of amusement in his eyes. "And our little corner of this Mid-Atlantic paradise?"

"Has cumulus clouds, of course. They could be the precursors of more severe weather if their moisture content increases."

"We'll keep an eye out for storms, but for now I think we're safe."

From the weather, at least.

Frank guided the boat out of the marina and small harbor and into the open sea, pointing due north to his island. He engaged the autopilot system and slid open the windows on the bridge so they could catch the ocean breeze.

"So, Julia, tell me what you have been up to the past years. You must have spent a lot of time in school to get your graduate degree. Where did you go? Did you work at the same time?"

"Did I ever. Worked and worked." Julia sat in one of the swivel chairs and Frank sat across from her. Under his gentle questioning, she found herself telling him about her long years of nursing school in Boston, her first job in the E.R. that was both heartbreaking and exhilarating. "I went to graduate school because I wanted to know more. I got tired of wanting to know things that I didn't know and not knowing how to learn them."

"It sounds as if you must've learned plenty." Frank looked at the control panel again to make sure that they were still on the right course.

Julia wasn't sure that they were on the right path at all but it was kind of late to turn back now. But she decided to just go with the flow and see what happened.

"I hope you're hungry. I picked up something at the café for lunch. With working at the villa, Benedito and I didn't have time to cook anything today."

"Do you know how to cook?" If Julia's memory was correct, Frank knew how to open a bottle of wine and make sandwiches. Not that there was anything wrong with wine or sandwiches. She had pretty much lived on a diet of sandwiches while she was in school. And working in the E.R. meant that the cafeteria was closed at night, so she often lived on a diet of vending machine offerings. Of course Portuguese sandwiches were a lot nicer than the white bread and turkey slices of dubious origin that lurked in the hospital cafeteria.

"I made myself learn how to cook. Benedito's wife Leonor taught me several of her dishes. Although they don't taste the same but I often wonder if she left ingredients out on purpose. She is a rather jealous cook, you know." Frank stood up. "Are you thirsty? I have several soft drinks down in the galley if you're interested."

Julia realized her mouth was quite dry from all the talking. She had not talked that long with anybody for weeks, if not months. Her father never expected her to talk much, and her mother talked enough for all three of them. "Sure, I'd love a drink—a cola if you have one, with plenty of ice."

Frank jumped to his feet. "I'll be back in a minute."

Julia got up to stretch her legs and looked out one of the windows. She spotted a blue smudge on the far horizon rising out of the sea. It had to be Belas Aguas. Her mouth got even drier at the sight of the place where she and Frank had been so happy.

And there he was at her elbow, passing her a cold drink. His own drink was equally full but without the ice cubes. "I knew you were going to be on the boat," he said. "I laid in more ice than the local fishing fleet needs."

She elbowed him in the ribs with her free arm. "Warm soda is a sign of barbarism. What's the point in having warm drinks? If you want something warm, you should make yourself a pot of tea or coffee."

Frank winced. "Please tell me you don't refrigerate

your red wine." He looked around the bridge. "I may have to get myself a tissue since you'll make me cry."

Julia gave him a sweet smile. "Why, Frank, there's nothing better on a hot summer day than a glass of cold red wine. With ice cubes."

He groaned. "Now that is a sign of true barbarism. Do you know how hard we have to work to make an excellent red wine? Years and years. First we have to grow the grapes, then we have to harvest them. After that, we pull our hair out during fermentation, and then we pour it into the casks, hoping that it turns out to be something in several years." He rested his fingers lightly on her shoulder. "Please tell me you're joking."

"Of course I'm joking, Frank," she teased. "I only drink *white* wine with ice cubes."

"Ah, Julia, you do not give an inch, do you?" He looped his arm around her neck and pulled her to him unselfconsciously, planting a kiss on the top of her head. "Peaches." He sighed happily.

Just then, her stomach gave a terrible growl. He started to laugh, and she gave up and joined in. "Don't worry, honey, we're almost there." He pointed at the blue smudge in the distance that was becoming less of a smudge and more of a distinct shape with every minute that they drew closer.

He took one last drink of his cola and set it aside in the cup holder, his free arm still looped around her shoulder. "Time to put it back on manual control now. I'd hate to run aground on my own island. Rather embarrassing for me, don't you think?"

"And rather hard on us and the boat, as well." The island was turning from blue to green in front of her eyes. It was a longer, lower island than many of the others in the Azores, covered in stumpy trees and green, green grass. Since the temperatures were between the fifties and seventies year-round, nothing ever froze, unlike Boston.

Belas Aguas had always reminded her of a giant golf course, smooth and green. And terribly expensive. "Did you ever think about turning some of the land into a golf course?" she asked, knowing it was a nosy question.

"A golf course?" Frank started to laugh. "No, I can't say I ever considered that. At one point, we were thinking about renting out the villa to people who needed a private vacation spot."

"Like for your friend Stefania and her new husband." She tapped her fingers on the glass of cola. "I can see how that would work."

"Well, Belas Aguas isn't exactly a beach hotspot. We don't have a deep enough harbor to take really large ships, and the weather never gets really hot here unlike in the Mediterranean." He flipped a couple switches and took his arm off her shoulder so he could steer the boat. She moved away from him, disappointed, and that was not a good sign.

Julia had been counting on the presence of their elderly chaperon, Benedito. Not because *she* was afraid Frank would do anything, but because she was afraid that she might. Well, she'd just have to behave herself, despite all of Frank's signals that he would rather she did the opposite.

"So, STEFANIA HAS DECIDED to pick gold and ivory for her bridal colors. The cathedral in Vinciguerra has beautiful marble with lots of gold decoration and her wedding dress is ivory satin with gold trimming on it. The dress designer is engaged to my friend George, Stefania's brother. That's actually how they met. Since Stefania's parents are passed away, George, Jack and I offered to help her with her wedding plans." Frank knew he was babbling as he unlocked the kitchen door of the villa, but nerves were getting the best of him.

Julia nodded as she entered the kitchen. "Well, this certainly looks the same," she said.

He grimaced and she saw it. "No, that's not what I mean. I love the timelessness of the villa—of the whole island." She walked around the kitchen running her hands along the old wooden table that acted as a center island. "How old is this table?"

He shrugged, and set down the big paper bag of carry-out lunch from the café. "I suppose it's really old. Benedito says that it's been here since he was a boy, and he is at least 118 years old."

Julia laughed. "You two are so bad together, but I suppose by now it's just a game for you."

"He means well, and he takes joy in keeping me on my toes. No chance of me becoming a stuffy nobleman with Benedito around."

"You could never be stuffy, Frank."

"My father died when I was about eleven, and I became the Duke. My mother is a lovely woman, but with my father gone, she focused all her fussing on me. I was well on my way to becoming quite the insufferable little prig, striding around the *fazenda* and barking orders to the men. Benedito was the only one who dared say boo to me and he made it quite clear that while I may have inherited the title, I had to earn the respect that went along with it."

"I can't quite see you as the arrogant lord of the manor." She leaned against the table, the movement causing her cleavage to deepen.

"Here, let me take your jacket for you." It was a pretty spring-green color that looked wonderful with her dark hair and hazel eyes. Of course, she could be wearing an old horse blanket and he would still think she looked wonderful. Especially if that was all she was wearing.

Frank hung her jacket on a hook next to the door and forced himself to concentrate on their conversation. "Oh, I was a real piece of work at that age. Riding boots, a small riding crop and a bad attitude to go with them both."

"But your father just died," she said. "Anybody would've had a hard time with that, especially a boy of that age."

"And that's why Benedito didn't beat the, um, snot out of me. He just worked me until I was too exhausted to be obnoxious."

"Attitude correction through exhaustion. I can think of a few nurses that I would like to try that technique on. Most emergency room nurses are good team players, but there are always a few prima donnas in any group."

Frank took out a container that smelled delicious—maybe beef? He'd offered the cook at the café a small fortune to make a wonderful meal for two. It looked as if it was enough food for five. "Are you hungry?" He had finished unpacking the one bag and went to the next. This bag had those tasty marinated olives and more pastries. He hoped they would put her in an equally sweet mood.

"Starving," she said. "I only had some fruit and bread

and butter for breakfast, and after that I was in the hair salon all morning." She looked mortified, as if she hadn't meant to tell him about that part of her day.

Frank hid a smile. His masculine nature puffed up in the knowledge that she had spent her whole morning primping for him. "It was time well spent," he said. "But you do realize that I have always enjoyed your looks, hairstylist or not."

"Good thing for me," she retorted, "because I am not sure I can do this again myself." She pulled a curl in front of her nose and deliberately looked at it cross eyed.

He couldn't help laughing. She was the most unpretentious woman he'd known. Unlike Paulinha, who needed at least three hours to get ready for a simple evening, and six for a formal function. He tensed briefly and deliberately shoved away her image. He hadn't ever promised her anything, but once he went back to Portugal, he had to make his intentions—or lack of intentions—clear. It wasn't fair to her, taking time away from her life in Lisbon to travel to Aguas Santas, presumably to visit with his sister.

And compared to Julia's tart sense of humor and lack of deference, Paulinha was almost too sweet, like eating a box of pastries all by himself. When he was younger, he had basked in her girlish admiration as a balm to his battered ego, but now she was a woman and rightfully expected the things a woman expected of an eligible single man.

Things he wasn't willing to give. At least to her.

"Why so serious?" Julia gave him a playful squeeze on the back of his arm. "Did the café pack the wrong food?"

"No, of course not." He busied himself unloading the bags and pulled several serving bowls out of a cabinet.

Julia opened a box and inhaled deeply. "Mmm, pork." She started to pour it into a bowl and Frank shooed her away.

"No, no, you are my guest. If you would like to freshen up before lunch, the powder room is through that door and on the left."

"Okay, if you insist." She strolled off and he hurried to fill the bowls. The dining room table was already set, so all he had to do was open a bottle of Aguas Santas red wine and let it sit for a few minutes before pouring it.

He set the bowls on the table, which would easily hold a dozen guests, but he had set places across from each other at one end. No point in creating the old farce where the couple yelled at each other from opposite ends of a giant table. The dishes were heavy pottery instead of fine china, but Frank wanted to keep things looking casual. The red, yellow and blue glaze had a warm, friendly Mediterranean look that said, *Just a casual lunch between friends. No, really, I'm not trying to get you into bed. I'd use the good china for that.*

He groaned. Ever since he'd been helping Stefania with her bridal registry, he'd learned more about china and dishes than any red-blooded man needed to know.

"Frank?" Julia called, a funny tone in her voice.

"Are you all right?" He stopped worrying about dishes and trotted down the hallway to the powder room. She stood in the doorway, a pained expression on her face.

"I'm all right, but your bathroom is coming down with something."

"What?" He stuck his head in the door. "What!" Wide swathes of violent acid green and pumpkin orange striped the walls.

"So this isn't your redecoration attempt?"

He shoved his hands into his hair and gripped his scalp. "Benedito! Oh, my God, why would he do this?"

"He's testing the paint colors to see which looks better." Julia tried fighting back a laugh and gave up. She laughed so hard that she bent at the waist, gripping the sink to hold herself upright.

"Testing the paint colors?" Frank stared at the wall in horror. "Look better?"

Julia started to cough from laughing. "Oh, Frank, this is the worst…" She broke into giggles again.

"He actually bought these colors." He was in that state of shocked amazement where it wasn't quite sinking in.

She hauled herself upright. "You better check the rest of the villa."

His jaw dropped. "Oh, dear God." He bolted into the living room. Fortunately Benedito had left the exposed stone and white plaster alone. He thumped upstairs to the master suite, which was the other focus of the re-do.

"Red?" he howled. The bubblegum pink had been bad enough, but Benedito had taken the opportunity while Frank was busy outside to try out three different shades of red on the wall next to the bathroom. It looked as if they had been slaughtering livestock, only messier, thanks to the drops that had run down the wall.

Julia came up behind him. "Trying for the romantic look?"

"Probably reminded him of a brothel in Lisbon from his bachelor days," he said without thinking.

She burst out laughing again. "Oh, Frank, what were you thinking to let him pick colors?"

"Let him? Let him? I've been trying to get him to the eye doctor for the past year to check his cataracts! He told me after the fact that he had bought paint so I could have more time with you."

"Aww." Julia wiped a tear from the corner of her eye. "That's sweet."

"Sweet? I have to paint over this and get new paint. Do you know how much primer that will take?"

"For a second I thought I was back in the E.R." She made a face. "What color were you going to paint this room?"

He made a helpless gesture. "Off-white? I thought *I* was bad with decorating, but..."

"We'll figure this out," she announced. "I decorated my own condo a few years back—no problem." Her stomach growled. "Is lunch ready?"

"I'll need to open another bottle of wine." He shook his head and followed her downstairs. What a mess. On the other hand, Julia had offered to help him, so that meant more time with her. Maybe Benedito had this in mind the whole time. If so, he'd pull a bottle of the 1958 sherry out of the *fazenda's* cellar and give it to the old man with a big, fat kiss.

6

JULIA PUSHED AWAY FROM THE lunch table and groaned. The café had outdone itself again with a pork stew, spiced beef and garlicky roasted potatoes. She'd allowed herself a glass of Frank's own red wine but had sipped on it through several courses along with mineral water so she wouldn't get a headache.

"More dessert?" He offered her a cream-filled pastry, but she shook her head.

"No. I'm so full, thanks." She stood, enjoying the slight dizziness that came with good food and wine, not head injuries.

Frank jumped to his feet, as well. He may have been the descendant of autocratic peasant-repressers, but he did have nice manners. She gathered up her plate and he made such a dismayed sound that she nearly dropped it. "What?"

"You are my guest." He snatched it away from her. "Guests never need to clear their own plates. I'll take care of this." He shooed her away and Julia realized she did need to use the facilities. Unfortunately that meant the pumpkin-pistachio powder room of horrors, but she hadn't drunk enough that it made her physically ill. Just visually.

She finished and washed her hands as quickly as possible before returning to the kitchen. The kitchen was her favorite room in the whole villa, even before the paint fiasco. It had probably been the only room for many years judging from its size and the giant fireplace. Julia could imagine the hearth heating the space, with big tables and plenty of room for a bed tucked into the corner next to the fireplace. Even now, there was a leather sofa in front of the hearth, the substantial island and a dark rustic table that would easily seat ten. She'd seen reproductions on furniture websites but Frank's table was the real deal, probably made from wood shipped from the mainland several hundred years ago.

Frank had turned on the radio he kept on the kitchen counter and listened to rapid-fire Portuguese. His frown deepened. Julia looked out the window and knew what was coming. She couldn't understand the radio, but she knew weather from her life on air force bases.

She stuck her head out the back door. The sunny day had rapidly darkened, with ominous clouds blowing from the west. It had been such a warm day and a cold front was stirring up trouble when it hit the mass of warm air. Ah, life on an island.

This storm was a bad one, and they would be foolish to set off for the bigger island of São Miguel.

He turned down the volume and faced her. "Julia, the weather has turned, and there is a boating danger advisory. I can't take you back. You'll have to spend the night."

Her stomach quivered. A night in the villa with

Franco was laden with possibilities—and pitfalls. He stared at her and she knew he felt the same way. "I have to spend the night," she echoed. "With you."

"With me." He took a step closer. "Don't worry, *meu bem*. I will take care of you."

Meu bem. That was hard to translate into English but easy to understand, basically meaning "sweetheart."

"I trust you, Frank." She touched his cheek and he covered her hand with his, turning his face to kiss her palm.

"Maybe you shouldn't." He dropped her hand and spun away. "I have to check on the boat."

His steps echoed on the stone floor as he hurried out the door down to the dock. She slowly lowered her hand to her side, her palm burning where he kissed it. The rest of her burned as well.

Julia redirected her attention. A storm on a small island meant loss of utilities, so she searched in the kitchen cabinets and pantry for flashlights, candles, matches and even kerosene lanterns. After setting several of each on the center island, she filled several jugs with tap water and then ran both the downstairs and upstairs bathtubs full to use for flushing and bathing, if needed. As the tub filled upstairs, she glanced around the master suite, noting the dated overblown cabbage rose décor and baby pink bathroom, not to mention the red paint samples. No wonder Frank wanted to update the villa before his young friend's honeymoon.

Frank's comb and brush sat on the white spindly dressing table, complete with gilded mirror. A dark blue T-shirt hung over the gold-velvet upholstered chair. She couldn't imagine Frank enjoyed sleeping there in that

ugly bed. Poor Frank, under that dizzying bedspread.
Some impulse made her test the mattress with her hand.

Frank all alone. Naked. His smooth skin catching on
the worn sheets as he tossed and turned, his cock hardening in the night. He would toss the bedding away and
cup himself, erect and thick. She swallowed painfully,
desire thickening her blood. Her nipples tightened as
she fantasized about him caressing himself from base
to tip.

Juices slipping from him as they were slipping from
her. She moaned, the pulsing between her thighs unbearable enough that she rubbed herself through her
thin denim pants. A poor substitution for a real man,
but the pull of her fantasy was too much to stop.

His fingers caressing his hard, masculine nipples.
She undid a button and slipped her hand inside her
blouse. Her breasts were full and heavy, their peaks
aching as she tentatively brushed across them.

His hands tightening around his dark, heavy sac,
milking and stroking himself. His heels digging into
the mattress as his back arched from the bed, his hands
working himself into a powerful frenzy of desire. Up
and down his shaft.

"Oh, yes," she moaned, shivering at the edge of
orgasm. Her hand crept up toward the drawstring at
her waist. One touch on her bare flesh and she would
shatter.

Him crying out in pleasure. Calling her name in violent climax—*Julia, Julia.*

"Julia! Julia!" The call was real this time. She yelped
and yanked her hands from her body.

She blindly pulled extra blankets and pillows from
the linen closet next to the bathroom. She headed for

the stairs and almost knocked both of them down the rest of the way.

"Careful, Julia." He steadied her and took the pile from her. "Downstairs with these?"

"Yes." Her face was burning and her breath was as fast as if she had just played a soccer match.

"I saw all the supplies in the kitchen and the water as well. Good thinking. The electrical power still runs through that underwater cable from São Miguel, but the lines on our island are above ground and go down sometimes. If we lose electricity, we'll have some generator power but not enough to run the water pump very much."

She shivered, half from desire and half because the temperature had dropped precipitously. He noticed, but she had the feeling he noticed everything about her. "Go upstairs to the master suite where I'm staying. There should be a sweater in the closet. I'll bring these blankets downstairs."

Back to her fantasy room. She ducked in and grabbed a yellow fleece pullover that made her look like a hazard sign, even though she was still steaming hot. At least it was on the inside, where he couldn't see.

Frank had set the blankets on the big leather couch in front of the fireplace and was eyeing the iron firewood rack. "We don't have much wood inside. I'll go to the shed in back to bring more in."

"Do you need me to help?"

He laughed. "You're asking a Portuguese man if he wants a woman to help him with heavy lifting? Remember where you are."

"Hmmph." As if she could forget. "Would you like

me to cook or clean something while you do all the manly work around here?"

He gave her a long look up and down her body. "You make me wish I could do even more manly work for you." Then he disappeared out the kitchen door.

Wow. She stood for several long seconds staring after him and then shook herself and got to work. She did a quick inventory of the fridge and pantry, noting the leftovers from lunch, some eggs, sausage, bread and milk. If the power went out, she could cook the eggs over the fireplace in one of the well-seasoned cast iron skillets, maybe make some French toast or an omelet. The sausage was smoked, so no need to keep it cold. Everything would keep until breakfast tomorrow.

Julia slowly closed the refrigerator door, making sure it was snug. How long since she had shared breakfast with a man? And no, quick runs to the hospital cafeteria for leaden pancakes or stale Danishes after a hellacious night of work didn't count.

She thought. And thought. And thought. And decided to stop thinking after she had traveled well back into the previous decade.

But before breakfast came the night together. The pile of bedding drew her gaze.

Frank thumped through the door balancing an armful of firewood. He set the logs in the wrought-iron holder and then winced and shook his hand.

"What is it?"

"Splinter." He picked at his palm with and then winced again. "Ah, I only got part of it."

"Let me see." She took his hand in hers. "Look, you broke it off inside and drove it even deeper."

"Good thing I have a trained nursing professional to treat me," he teased her.

"I don't know how good of a thing it is. I'm pretty rusty since I've been off work for several weeks," she joked back. His hand was warm and heavy in hers, his fingertips thickened from hard work but smooth, as if he took the effort to care for them.

They would be just the right combination of rough and smooth over her skin. Her fingers tightened on his briefly and she forced herself to relax.

"Hey, don't worry. I'm sure you'll be able to manage."

So he thought she was nervous about taking out his splinter instead of holding his hand. "Where do you keep your first aid supplies?"

"What first aid supplies?" He looked around in confusion. "I don't think we have any. We just usually use soap and adhesive bandages. We are hearty people and don't need much."

"Frank!" she scolded him. "You live on an island forty minutes by boat from the nearest hospital. You don't need to keep blood plasma in your refrigerator, but some basic supplies could save somebody's life."

"Julia, Julia." He roared with laughter and yanked her into his arms, nuzzling her hair. "Of course we have supplies. I wouldn't let my mother and sisters and all those nieces and nephews stay out here with only soap and adhesive bandages. We even have one of those electronic heart defibrillators and were all trained to use it."

"Hmmph," she muttered into his chest. "You are a terrible tease, Franco Duarte."

His laugh rumbled under her cheek. "I may be a terrible tease but you are a wonderful nurse." He kissed the top of her head. "I'll show you our first aid kit and you can tell me all the things we are missing."

"Okay." Somehow Julia didn't quite feel like leaving the warmth of his embrace to inventory supplies. Frank was solid and reassuring and made her feel safe for the first time in months, despite warnings of storms and power outages. But he did have that splinter still lodged in his palm.

She forced herself to pull away. "Let's get you fixed up."

He raised his eyebrows and gave her an ironic half-smile, as if he knew she was running away from him. Or at least retreating strategically. "Come with me." He took her hand in his uninjured one and walked to the foyer. Along one wall was a large dark wood bench with a turkey-red padded rectangular cushion. Frank pulled off the cushion to reveal a hinged lid in the seat.

He reached inside a cutout hole and lifted it, revealing several large boxes nestled inside the bench. "Here we are. The defibrillator—" he pointed to a bright red plastic container "—and the other supplies." He pulled them out for her and she knelt down and eagerly opened them.

There was enough to take care of his splinter and much more. Compression bandages, regular bandages, antibiotics, painkillers, syringes, epinephrine pen injectors, even some bags of IV fluid and... "Ooh, blood clotting granules. These are wonderful! If you have a serious injury, you just sprinkle them in to stop the bleeding. That is so thoughtful of you, Frank."

He gave her an incredulous smile. "The most surprising things impress you, Julia. Not to brag, but here I am, one of the only dukes in Portugal, pretty well-off, moderately good-looking and owner of a big estate and my own island, and what impresses you about me? The fact that I have blood clotting granules in my first aid kit. You truly amaze me."

She shook a packet at him. "That other stuff is not life-and-death, Frank. This is."

"You're right. And I'll impress you however I can."

"You don't need to impress me."

"Don't I?" He lifted a black brow.

No, he didn't need to impress her. He always had. Even as a young man he had been kind and friendly to everyone, not at all arrogant like she had assumed a man of his position to be. Apparently after they'd first parted, he'd continued his education and learned almost every job on his estate so he could be a hands-on leader.

"Julia…" he murmured, raising his hand to cup her cheek. Fortunately she spotted the splinter before he could press it in farther.

"Geez, Frank, I have to get that out."

He rolled his eyes. "It's not like it's a gunshot wound, Julia."

She froze for a second and forced herself to relax. "No, it's not. But I know what to do with those, too."

"Really?" He gave her a sad look, his brown eyes darkening. "I suppose you would, working in a city emergency room. I'm sorry."

"What for?" She busied herself looking for the antiseptic wash and tweezers. "We can usually fix them up."

"Usually," he echoed.

"Not all the time," she allowed, standing up. "There's better light in the kitchen."

He realized she was trying to change the subject

and followed her obediently for once. At the kitchen sink, she made quick work of the splinter and washed and bandaged the small wound. "You've had a tetanus booster in the past ten years?"

He nodded. "I cut myself on some rusty barbed wire a few years ago and got one then." He rubbed his upper arm. "It made my arm hurt for three days."

"Then you should be all set." She let go of his hand but he stood there expectantly. "What?"

"Aren't you going to kiss it to make it better?"

"Frank..." She started to blush.

"It really hurts." He put on a pained look.

She doubted it. The antibiotic ointment had a small amount of numbing ingredients in it. "I don't kiss my patients."

He came closer and she backed up until she was practically sitting in the sink. But this time, she didn't feel panicked or closed in. After all, it was just Frank. "I've been very patient with you, Julia, but I'm not one of your patients."

"You're rather impatient, Frank." Just as she said that, their hips touched and she realized how impatient he was. His erection was obvious, even through his jeans, fitting perfectly into the cradle of her hips.

Her eyes widened and he nodded ruefully. "We've waited long enough, Julia. Won't you kiss me and make it all better?"

"Just your hand," she emphasized.

"For now." He rotated slightly, rubbing against her. She exhaled shakily. To feel all of that inside her...her fantasy from upstairs came roaring back and her nipples tightened against her thin bra.

But all he was asking for was a little kiss. On his

hand, even. She took his wrist and placed a kiss near his bandage.

"And here." He wiggled his fingertips.

"What? You're not hurt there."

"The pain is radiating outward."

She went along with him and kissed each fingertip, his skin catching a bit on the tender inner skin of her lips. He watched her eagerly, his pupils dilating until his eyes were almost black.

She nipped at his index finger and giving into the desire she'd tried to suppress all day, sucked it into her mouth. He groaned in shock and lust. "Julia…"

She swirled her tongue around his finger, the thick skin scraping along her nerve endings. She imagined doing the same thing to his erection that pressed between them.

He yanked his hand free and pulled her close. Just then, a huge clap of thunder startled them apart and a repetitive thumping noise came from outside. He bit out a Portuguese oath and craned his head toward the kitchen door. "Don't go anywhere. I'll be right back." He bent down and gave her a fierce, fast kiss before tossing on a rain slicker.

She clutched the countertop, her heart pounding. What had possessed her to be so bold? She hadn't made up her mind to make love with Frank—had she?

Julia slumped onto a stool. Maybe she had. She'd seen the clouds coming from the west, had seen the waves starting to rise as they'd boated to Frank's island. Her psychology class wasn't much more than a distant memory, but even she could remember the pesky subconscious part of the mind that knew a person's hidden wishes and cheerfully shoved her along toward attaining them.

Stupid Freud. Stupid subconscious. She'd known the weather would likely go bad and she'd be stranded on the island in the middle of a storm.

How very gothic of her. All she had to do was run screaming into the night with the Duke of Aguas Santas chasing her and they'd be reenacting one of those novels her mother had devoured when Julia was a kid. Except Julia had never grown up to be as buxom as those heroines.

On the other hand, Frank apparently still thought she was fine in the buxom department. And she was pretty sure he had absolutely no interest in running around his island in a thunderstorm in the dark, given how he'd cursed before going outside to fix whatever was thumping.

He was obviously interested in staying indoors with a nice fire, a bottle of wine and a heaping helping of soft bedding.

Her eyes strayed to the pile of blankets. It did make sense to stay downstairs since their only heat source was the fireplace.

She snorted. Oh, yes, that wouldn't be their only heat source.

The lights went off and a dark figure stood in the door, silhouetted by lightning. Julia let out a piercing shriek that surprised even herself.

"*Ay, caramba!* Julia?"

"Frank?"

"Who else would it be?" He came into the kitchen and she shrunk back until she could see his face lit up by the next lightning bolt.

"Oh. Hi, Frank."

"Hi, Frank?" he echoed. "You scared the life out of me. *Meu Deus,* oh, my God. My heart is pounding."

"Good thing we have the defibrillator."

"Very funny." He shucked his jacket and hung it up on a hook near the door. "As I was planning to tell you before we started our little horror movie reenactment—"

Julia couldn't help giggling.

"What's so funny?" He came closer, flipping the wet hair out of his eyes.

"While you were out, I was thinking that we were reenacting a gothic novel."

"Eh?"

"Dark, stormy nights, vulnerable maidens being chased by the lord of the manor."

"That does sound more fun than my idea," he admitted. "What does the lord of the manor do to the vulnerable maiden when he catches her?"

"Frank!" She was happy he couldn't see her blushing.

He sighed. "Well, if you've ruled out the chase scene, let's light some candles." He pulled out some matches from next to the fireplace and lit several candles as well as a lantern. With the additional light, she saw it wasn't just his hair that was wet.

"That raincoat didn't do you much good—you're wet down to the skin."

He shrugged. "The door on the outbuilding blew open and broke a pane of glass when it hit. I was standing right under the gutter overflow trying to fix the latch and the water ran down my back. I'll dry out soon, especially once I get this fire going." He knelt at the hearth and patiently coaxed the kindling and smaller logs to full flame.

"That looks great. Now will you go change?"

"Fine, fine," he grumbled, snagging a lantern to take upstairs. "Don't go anywhere. I don't feel like chasing you across the yard, however literary it would be."

He went upstairs and she frantically patted her hair down, but the humidity was wreaking its vengeance on her for daring to try to straighten it. She gave up and finger-curled a few strands around her face.

And anyway, they were using candles and firelight, and didn't every woman look better in that light? She looked down at her ruffled blouse, which was as droopy as her hair was puffy.

Was she keeping it on or taking it off? She realized Frank hadn't brought her to his island specifically for making love, but it seemed as if the opportunity was presenting itself.

He reappeared in the doorway from the hall. She nearly swallowed her tongue at the sight. He wore old gray sweatpants riding low on his hips, a white towel slung around his neck—and nothing else. The firelight turned his skin to molten gold, the dark hair on his chest narrowing into a delicious line pointing south. All that separated her from him was a tug of the elastic. She had the sneaking suspicion he was flying solo underneath his pants, so to speak.

"Are you comfortable now?" she managed, reaching for her glass of wine to moisten her mouth.

"No, I am not, Julia." As she stared at him, his waistband started to shift and pull with his arousal, making it very obvious how she affected him. Her jaw fell.

She dragged her gaze up to his face.

He shrugged ruefully. "I cannot help it. I could put on different clothing to hide my desire for you, but we would both know the truth. I am not ashamed that I want you, and I believe you want me, as well."

Her jaw dropped the rest of the way at his blunt speaking. "I…uh, well, uh…" She couldn't stop sneaking looks at his perfectly sculpted body. His body that was walking toward her. No, make that stalking toward her.

"You feel it, too, don't you? Even stronger than before."

"Yes," she whispered.

"Then I am yours tonight." He tossed the towel aside. "Do with me what you will." He stopped in front of her, heat and maleness radiating off him.

But that was all he did, despite how his pants were buckling under the strain. She understood that the choice was entirely hers. Yes, she was stranded on his island and totally under his physical control. He could do anything he wanted to her and she would be helpless to resist. Helpless to resist his touch, his mouth, his seduction. She let out a little groan at the images that conjured up. Maybe her fantasy of being chased and captured wasn't just an idle one.

But she understood why he was making her decide. He had always left the choice up to her. Even when he should have chased after her.

Julia didn't want any more lost opportunities. She reached out to touch his cheek. "I want you, too, Franco."

He closed his eyes in what looked almost like relief. He cupped her wrist and nuzzled her palm. "Then what are we waiting for?"

He sat on the leather couch and guided her to sit on his lap. He was full and hard against her bottom, but contented himself with kissing her cheek and jaw. "So soft, so smooth." He rested his forehead on hers. "Julia, it's been so long."

She put her finger on his lips. "Let's leave the past in the past. Tonight, everything is new. *We* are new."

"Agreed." She thought she saw relief in his eyes. He didn't want to get into the mess they'd made in the past any more than she did.

Tonight it was easier to think of him as a sexy Portuguese guy she'd met while on a fun Azores vacation. Kind of like the first time they'd met. Why didn't she have any more sense now? Shouldn't she be the sadder but wiser girl at this point?

But Julia mentally put the brakes on that line of thinking. She might not be any wiser, but tonight would sure make her happier, as evidenced by Frank's clever fingers delicately undoing her buttons.

Her gaze locked with his as he finished opening her blouse and pulled it open. She sat quietly as he pushed it off her shoulders. No hurrying for them tonight.

Frank stroked her cheek and slid his fingers into her hair, gently bringing her mouth to his. She closed her eyes as his lips met hers.

Pure heaven. Tears pricked her eyelids, and she hoped they didn't fall and earn his notice. She took a deep breath and fell into his kiss, warm and tender.

He moved his mouth over hers, nipping and sucking at her lips, kissing her cheeks as he cupped her face. She rested her hands on his shoulders, enjoying the play of muscles under his silky skin. He had definitely gained strength and power since she had last held him in her arms, but of course, that was to be expected. Eleven years had developed him from a young kid just leaving his teens to a mature, powerful man.

And she had missed all of it. Someone else had witnessed the fulfillment of his manhood. If things had turned out badly for her when she was injured, she never would have seen him again.

He stopped abruptly.

"What?" She opened her eyes hazily and realized he was wiping tears off her face. "Oh, um…" Her throat closed up.

"Julia, *amor meu.*" He shook his head. "We do not have to do this if you are not ready."

The floodgates opened and she buried her face in his neck. He leaned back into the sofa and wrapped his arms around her, murmuring soothing things in Portuguese.

She cried for all the lost years and all the stupid dates she had been on with losers and nice guys whose only problem was that they weren't Francisco Duarte. Cried for all the time she'd spent grieving over losing him and kicking herself for not being brave enough to drive a couple hours to New York to see him.

He sat patiently under her until she ran out of tears, handing her a tissue from a box next to the couch. "Julia, you are breaking my heart." He was telling the truth; she could hear the pain in his voice. "Tell me, my princess, what makes you cry so?"

She debated what to tell him. "Being here with you is very emotional."

"Tell me about it," he murmured, his dark eyes looking a bit wet themselves.

"When I got hurt at work, a patient in the emergency

room was giving us trouble and I got caught in the middle. He shoved me into the countertop and I hit my head—pretty good concussion."

"A head injury? My God, why didn't you tell me?" He examined her scalp with his fingers and she pointed to the area that had been injured. "Does it still hurt?"

She shook her head. "No more headaches, but I feel almost…raw. Like when you have a healing scar and the skin is new and pink and tender. Concussions can make people moody."

"Oh, dear." His mouth pulled into a small smile. "But I know how to help moody women. I have four younger sisters—five if you count Stefania. Would you like some Belgian chocolate?"

She burst out laughing. "Frank, you dope. I had a head injury, not PMS."

He gave her a bigger grin and she realized that he had succeeded in cheering her up. "You can still have the chocolate."

But he wouldn't make the next move. It was Julia who needed to start things up again. "Let's have chocolate later, after we work up an appetite."

"I already have a big appetite," he murmured seductively, his erection firming under her again.

"Why don't you show me?"

Frank hastily tossed the blankets in front of the fireplace and guided Julia down with him so they knelt face-to-face. She stroked his chest. His fingers quickly undid the catch and peeled her bra away.

"Beautiful." He cupped her breasts, her plump flesh pale against his strong brown hands. He brushed each nipple until they stood up in tight peaks, then rolled them between his thumbs and forefingers.

She arched into his touch, desperately wanting him to ease the throbbing between her thighs.

But he was determined to take his sweet time, and nuzzled her hair aside to nibble her neck.

"Frank," she moaned, wrapping her arms around him.

"Mmm." He nipped at her earlobe. "Don't you like this, my darling Julia?"

She shivered at both his exquisite torture and his endearment. "Love it."

He tongued the hollow behind her ear. "Then let's keep going." He pinched her nipple, and she was powerless to resist.

"Keep going."

He sat back against the couch and moved her rubbery legs so she straddled his muscular thigh. She settled onto him and gasped at the pressure against her clit. Without meaning to, she began grinding on him as he played with her breasts.

"Oh, yes, that's it," he crooned. "Poor Julia, you've missed my touch, haven't you?"

She nodded.

"My hands, my cock, my mouth?" He leaned forward and imprisoned a nipple deep in his mouth and she screamed in pleasure. He was hot and wet as he sucked on her, stroking her with his tongue and even biting her gently.

She tried to undo her pants but he easily caught her hands and held them behind her back. "Not yet. I want to make you come like this."

"But Frank," she whimpered. "Don't you want to come inside me?" It was a rhetorical question since his sweatpants were about to pull apart at the seams.

He gave a strained laugh. "When I push inside you, I want you so hot, so ready that you'll come as fast as I will. Now lean forward so I can suck on your juicy tits."

Her clit quivered at his sexy words. Even as a younger man, he'd enjoyed talking dirty to her and telling her in explicit detail what he was going to do to her and what she could do to him. It had always turned her on and tonight was no exception.

She surrendered and pressed her body into his. He immediately mouthed her other breast, but forgot something. "Frank?"

"Mmm." The suction was exquisite, hard enough to drive her crazy but not painful.

"Ah...my arms are still behind my back."

He let go. "Am I hurting you?"

"No, but..."

"You don't like the lack of control." He was too perceptive for his own good.

She shook her head.

"But, Julia, if I let go, you might start playing with your breasts, running your hands down to your wet little pussy to ease its ache," he explained matter-of-factly. "You are *my* guest on *my* island and I plan to do *everything* for you tonight. All night long."

"You brute," she said weakly, little shudders of desire rising from listening to him.

"I am. And we are alone in the middle of a storm where nothing but the wind will hear your screams of pleasure."

Hypnotized, she leaned forward, offering herself to him. He easily encircled her wrists with one hand and cupped the other breast. "Such soft skin," he murmured.

"Like silk. Like cream." He leaned forward and blew on her, raising goosebumps as he cooled her overheated flesh. She groaned.

"Don't you like this, darling?"

"Too much."

"It's never too much. It has never been enough, has it?"

Julia shook her head. Somehow, he still knew what she wanted, even when she didn't realize it herself.

He kissed along her collarbone. "I think you like your arms pinned behind your back. I think you like your breasts pushed out for me to touch." His strong fingers stroked and teased her skin, circling around but not touching the peaks. "For me to kiss." He bent his black head and kissed each nipple delicately. "For me to make love." He rolled a tip between his fingers.

She couldn't help herself and started riding his thigh again. "That's it, Julia." He pinched her a bit harder. "Use me for your pleasure. You've needed this for a long time." He sucked her other nipple and then blew on it. "Needed *me* for a long time."

She ground her hips hard into him, stunned at herself. Topless, riding his thigh with several layers of clothing with her hands trapped. Offering herself up to him totally.

It was his voice. His dark, sherry-accented voice luring her into his sensual intoxication. She was drunk with lust—no other explanation.

"Ride me, Julia. I can feel your hot, wet center burning me." He sucked on her nipples after that, biting, teasing her until she bucked on him, her head tossed back.

Dizziness spiraled around her, twisting up from her

pulsing clit to where their hands were locked together to where his mouth tormented her throbbing breasts. They were a whirlwind together, more powerful than the storm outside. She closed her eyes and let her climax sweep her away on a wave of intense pleasure. She dimly realized she was screaming his name into the storm, reveling in his possession of her.

After an eternity, she felt him release her arms and he lowered her to their nest of blankets. He pulled the rest of their clothing off and settled between her legs.

Her eyes flew open. "But what about protection?" Thank goodness she had remembered at literally the last minute.

He guided her hand down to his rock-hard cock, sheathed in latex. "Already taken care of." He nudged her thighs wider. "Take me inside you, Julia. I die for you."

She gladly accepted him, and they groaned simultaneously. Oh, my God, he was still built like a bull, even thicker and longer than she remembered. The walls of her passage eagerly squeezed him, and he began to move.

"So hot and tight," he gasped.

She dug her fingers into his shoulders and wrapped her thighs around his waist, not letting for an instant. "Do me hard, Franco."

He threw his head back in shock and stared down at her. She had never been the one to talk dirty, but judging by how he swelled and jumped within her, he liked it. "You want me to do what?" His voice was hoarse with desire.

Ah, he wanted her to say it again. "I want you to

do me hard, Franco. Now and all night, until I drain you dry."

He started slamming into her. "What else?"

She had to stop and think for a second. His luscious cock was heating her up again, especially when he slipped his hand between them and teased her clit. What else would she like him to do? Everything. Anything. One fantasy came to mind. "I want you to lick me."

"Where? Here?" He licked her neck. "Or here?" He licked her breast. "Or here?" He slowly pulled out of her, teasing her opening with his blunt tip and laughed as she clutched at him. "Oh, yes, *there*."

"Yes, there."

"Tell me, Julia. You want me to lick you where? You know my little secret now, that I like to hear you tell me naughty things. Be a naughty girl and tell me."

Her face was burning hot but he probably couldn't tell that in the firelight. "I want you to lick my pussy."

"Oh, I will." His promise was so heartfelt, she forgot her embarrassment. "I'll sit you in a chair and spread your soft thighs, kneel in front of you like a servant and sing your praises with my mouth."

"Oh, yes…" She arched under him and he stroked her tight little nub again and again, stretching her and filling her. His bronzed skin glistened in the firelight, his head tossed back in passion.

"Tell me you're close," he ground out. She nodded, gasping at his fat tip and thick shaft twisting inside her. Her insides were on fire, pulsing and trembling with his every stroke. He pinched her clit hard and she screamed in pleasure, shaking and falling apart underneath him.

He exploded into her, a hoarse cry spilling from his

lips. His frantic thrusts spurred her into another climax, her breath catching in her throat as she saw stars. He collapsed on top of her and they lay locked together, shuddering from orgasmic aftershocks.

He rolled to his side after a minute and took her with him, his cock still full and juicy inside her. "Oh, Julia, that was amazing."

Lying draped over him, she had to agree. "It's still early. We have plenty of time tonight."

He kissed her gently. "Why only tonight? Why not longer?"

She thought for a second. She didn't have any plans, and she was alone in the islands with no one to fuss at her. "What did you have in mind?"

"This." He brushed his fingertip over her clit and she shuddered in lust. "And more. Stay with me. I'll work on the renovations, you can sunbathe in the nude. I can watch you sunbathe, forget the renovations and make love to you next to the pool. Or on the beach. Or in the house. In a chair," he said with a devilish grin, reminding her of her fantasy. "Anything you want. And I mean *anything*."

"Anything?" That sounded slightly scary but delicious.

"Whenever you want. Or whenever I want," he added. "You and I, we are fantastic together. When will life again give us this opportunity?"

He had a good point. Life was so unpredictable.

"Wouldn't you like, just for once, to be a total hedonist? We eat what we want, we drink what we want. If we want to be naked all day, who cares? We can swim naked, lie in the sun, drink wine and make love to each other. Hell, do all of that at the same time."

"All right," she said slowly. "It sounds wonderful, but what about the end of our hedonism?"

He shrugged with a Mediterranean fatalism. "We see what happens then. *Carpe diem* as my Roman ancestors used to say. 'Seize the day.'"

"Seize the day." How many days had slipped away while she was slogging through her gray life in Boston? Over four thousand. What was a week or ten days if she could live them like this? "Yes, Frank, I'll stay with you here. But if either one of us has had enough, that's it."

"Of course. Along with oppressing peasants, we gave up kidnapping beautiful maidens a long time ago." He kissed her again. "You can go back whenever you want. But I hope not too soon."

"You've got a deal." She kissed him back, having the conflicting feelings of both coming home and standing at the edge of a precipice.

7

THE NEXT MORNING DAWNED bright and sunny. Julia yawned and stretched in their nest of blankets. Frank was nowhere to be seen, but she figured he was probably outside checking any storm damage. He was such a creature of the outdoors, unhappy if cooped up for too long inside. Unless, of course, he was distracted by something more interesting.

She sat up and giggled, giddy as a teenager with her first crush, but satisfied as only an adult woman could be. She rolled her neck and tentatively touched her hair, amazed to find that although messy, it wasn't wildly frizzy. Good grief, what did those women put in it? She didn't know whether to be pleased or worry that she would need the hair equivalent of paint stripper to wash the product out.

Ah, well, too nice a day to worry about hair gel. She needed to find something to wear so she could cook up a big breakfast for Frank. He'd be hungry.

She found her top but not her bra, her pants but not her underwear. A theme. She wrapped up in a sheet and headed for the bathroom with her available clothing.

If Frank was serious about having her stay, she'd need to make a trip back to her parents' apartment for more things. And she'd need to call them so they wouldn't worry about her disappearing for several days.

Julia grimaced. It had been a long time since she'd needed to check in with her parents, but they deserved the courtesy of knowing where she was. They worried a bit more than they used to. She'd make it sound as if there were a bunch of people working at the villa and she was doing it to keep from dying of boredom rather than dying of lust.

She hopped in the upstairs shower for a quick wash but was in the kitchen a few minutes later chopping up Portuguese sausage, onions, chives, peppers and tomatoes. She heated some olive oil in a skillet and tossed the mix in to start cooking down. The day-old crusty bread was perfect for French toast, so she beat a bunch of eggs, added cinnamon and a spoonful of sugar so the bread would brown nicely.

She soaked the bread in the egg mix and began frying the slices. The vegetable mix went into a yellow ceramic bowl. She wanted to wait for Frank to cook the omelets, since reheated eggs were terrible.

Almost forgot the coffee. It was perking along nicely when Frank came in a couple minutes later. He sniffed the air appreciatively. "What is that amazing smell?" He was amazing himself in a plain black T-shirt, khaki work pants and heavy workboots, which he toed off and left at the doormat. The T-shirt outlined all his chest muscles and he looked like a sexy, brawny construction worker.

"Coffee, French toast and I'll make you an omelet

if you'd like." It was so cozy and domestic that she couldn't stop grinning.

"Julia, you are a wonder." He caught her around the waist and kissed her. "Good morning, my darling."

She felt herself blush. "Good morning, honey." She hadn't used an endearment with anyone in years and it sounded stilted on her tongue, but he didn't notice and beamed at her.

"Oh, the French toast!" She rescued it just in time to flip and he poured them both a cup of coffee. "How did the island do with the storm?"

"Eh, we didn't do too badly." She thought it was cute how he referred to himself and the island as a pair. "Some branches down, a door blown off a garden shed, but I got the electricity going again."

"Isn't that dangerous?"

He shrugged. "I've done it many times. No big deal."

He'd think it was a big deal if he got shocked, but try telling him that now. She shook her head and pulled the French toast off, popping it into the oven to keep warm. "Ready for an omelet?"

"Always." He grinned at her and raised his cup of coffee in a toast.

A couple minutes later, they were sitting at the center island eating breakfast together. Maple syrup wasn't a staple in Portuguese houses, so they used local honey and jam for the French toast instead. "I really like pineapple jam on this," she told him, cutting a bite.

He grabbed her wrist and ate the bread off her fork. "I agree."

She shook her head in amusement and cut another piece. "Eat your own food. Didn't I make enough?"

"It tastes better coming from you." His big brown eyes melted her heart.

She sliced a bit of omelet and offered it to him. "Delicious," he said, after chewing and swallowing. "Here." He gave her some French toast with orange marmalade and honey. The tartness and sweetness mixed perfectly.

They fed each other the rest of breakfast. Julia dabbed at the corner of his mouth with her napkin. "You have honey here."

"So do you."

"I do?" She touched her mouth.

"Pure honey. But not from the jar." He moved her hand away and kissed her.

He cleared the dishes into the sink with a rattle and set her on the wood table. "All throughout breakfast, I've been watching your breasts sway, your dark nipples hardening against the fabric when you fed me." He slid his hand up her blouse and smiled when he found her bare breast. "Naughty Julia, where is your bra?"

She gestured helplessly at the tumbled blankets on the floor. "I couldn't find it."

"I'm not complaining." He unbuttoned her blouse and pushed it off her shoulders.

She automatically covered herself, not being used to daytime nudity. He made a chiding sound and pulled her arms away. "You're equally beautiful in the sun as the firelight." He rested his cheek against her heart. His hair was warm and silky on her skin. Her arms came around him and she twined a black wave around her finger. He smelled of wind and water and his own unmistakable spicy scent.

"Oh, Julia." He turned his face and kissed her breast. "Let me please you."

"You already do," she murmured. She felt him smile against her skin.

"A few years ago, I found several personal diaries of the previous Dukes of Santas Aguas. They discovered rather interesting ways to pass the time when they visited this island."

"They took up tennis?" she quipped.

He laughed. "More of an indoor activity. They would sail to São Miguel and find the prettiest young women on the island, then bring them back to Belas Aguas."

"To cook and clean?"

"To do whatever the Duke wanted."

He wasn't joking—she could tell this was a true story. "And they went along with this?"

Frank grinned. "It was considered an honor to have the attention of the Duke and he would send them back with a hefty dowry. The happier the girls made him, the bigger the dowry." He winked.

"What if the Duke didn't make *them* happy?"

"Oh, that was never an issue." He kissed her soft belly. "The young ladies were always very pleased with the Duke's particular skills." He circled his tongue around her belly button.

"But they couldn't go home." Her heart was pounding like crazy as he unbuttoned her denim pants.

He raised both eyebrows. "Did they want to? Back to washing and cooking and cleaning when they could be doing this?"

Julia automatically lifted her hips as he slid the capris off. The wood was surprisingly warm against her bare bottom.

He stroked a finger around her clit. "Do you want to go home? Shall I take you back?"

"No." She affected a disappointed sigh despite how his finger was driving her crazy. "Since you can't offer me a dowry, I suppose I can accept other means of exchange."

"I am grateful for your understanding. Perhaps I can make it up to you."

He stopped for a second and she opened her eyes in dismay. Her stare widened as he lifted the pot of honey. "Frank, what are you doing?"

"I am going to eat you up." He lifted the wooden spoon from the pot and drizzled the sticky liquid over her breasts. It was cool at first but quickly warmed and spread.

"Ooh, messy!"

He laughed. "By the time I'm done, you won't care." He dipped the spoon again and drew honey lines across her belly.

She lifted her head. "Is that an *F*?"

"*F* for *Frank,* of course." He raised his eyebrows at her. "What did you think? *F* for something else? Something you want me to do to you?"

He hadn't touched her directly but she was starting to shake with anticipation. She pressed her legs together to try to ease the ache between them, but he nudged them apart and dripped honey down her clit.

"Not because you're not sweet enough," he explained leisurely, as if he were working on a renovation project. "But because your hot little pussy will melt the honey and make you even slicker when I come to eat you up."

"Is this one of the secrets of the Dukes of Santas Aguas?" she asked.

"The mental aphrodisiac of a powerful nobleman

kneeling to pleasure a woman. You always found it extremely sexy, if I remember correctly."

"I did," she groaned, remembering how he had introduced her to the pleasures of oral sex, giving and receiving. She had been a virgin and he had been inexperienced as well, so they had learned together. Almost too well.

"Next time we'll lie down together. I'll lick your little honeypot and you can suck on me."

She shuddered in anticipation as more memories flooded to the surface. No wonder the Dukes of Santas Aguas had no problems attracting women to be their island sex slaves. She was no exception.

He replaced his finger with his mouth and she arched off the table. "Frank!"

He gave an amused hum and continued swirling his tongue around her clit, flicking and caressing it. She sobbed and clutched the edge of the table.

He slipped his finger inside her and she shuddered around him, slick and gripping. She moaned again and reached down to touch his hair. Tendrils of lust twined between her thighs, up her belly to her breasts. She fitfully brushed her nipple, hard and tight.

Frank lifted his head. "Cup your breasts, Julia. I want you to offer them up to me."

In a daze, she did as he asked. He rewarded her obedience, just as the previous Dukes of Santas Aguas rewarded their lovers—with pleasure, unbearable pleasure. He dipped his finger into the pot of honey and painted each nipple with a thick, sticky coating, his fingers playing and pinching each peak until they looked like glazed chocolate drops, shiny-brown and pointed.

"Sweet as candy, just for me."

"Touch me, Frank." She was sobbing by then at the empty ache between her thighs.

He shook his head and she brushed between her legs in desperation. "I said no." He caught her wrists in one big hand and held her arms over her head.

Her eyes widened, her hands trapped. "You're pinning me down." She meant it as a complaint, but her voice sounded more breathy and turned-on than anxious.

"Am I hurting you?" he asked, his voice dark with need.

She shook her head.

His gaze started at her flushed face and moved leisurely down to her honey-drenched breasts, down to her passion-drenched thighs. His cock pulsed against her hip. "Well, you're hurting me," he growled.

"You?"

"I hurt for you. My body is on fire and you are the only one who can save me." He fastened his mouth on her breast and she cried out again, the sweet, wet suction driving her mad. He licked the honey off her, nipping at the tip until she bucked under him. All he did was switch to the other breast, cleaning it with as much diligent attention as the first.

All the while he had her arms over her head, her breasts thrust upward for his greedy touch. She was at his mercy—but she loved it. Except she'd love it much better if he moved back down her body.

"Touch me, Frank," she begged.

"Where? Here?" He bent again, one hand on her breast and the other sliding down her body.

She tried to point but he shook his head. "Keep your

arms above your head or I'll wrap my belt around your wrists and tie you to the table."

She shuddered in pleasure and did as he asked. Imagining being tied up was an unexpected turn-on.

He reached her hot wet center and pushed a finger inside her. She arched off the table and he added another finger to thrust in and out, leisurely mimicking how he'd pleasured her last night. It was just as devastating, especially when he bent his head and sucked on her swollen little nub.

Dizzy heat burned through her and she thought she'd faint. His mouth teased and played with her, long licking strokes around mixed with sharp suction. Oh, yes, Frank was a master, and he was mastering her.

She reached down to touch his silky hair and he raised his head. "Ah, so you want me to tie you down?" His fingers continued their lazy strokes. "That big four-poster bed upstairs has seen more that its share of naughty women over the centuries. Imagine being tied up for unrelenting hours of passion as the Duke licked her, thrust into her, teased her. And only if she were very good, would he let her come." Frank pinched her nipple and Julia screamed his name, tension shattering inside of her as she climaxed.

He was between her thighs in an instant. She heard a packet crinkle and then he was spreading her wide open and sliding inside her. Her eyes flew open at his welcome invasion.

"Oh, yesss," he groaned. "Sticky, sweet and wet." He braced his hands on either side of her head. "Touch yourself, make yourself come again."

She reached between them, crying out as she found

her hot, swollen clit. She touched him too, brushing them both as she frantically rubbed herself.

"Yeah, I can feel you squeezing me." He sucked a honeyed nipple into his mouth and Julia screamed, coming again.

Frank moaned against her breast and exploded inside her, rocking the table with his frenzied thrusts. She clung to him, eagerly milking his cock for every last bit of pleasure. Both of their climaxes seemed to last for an eternity, but she finally opened her eyes. He gingerly raised himself up and pushed back to stand on the kitchen floor, quickly disposing of the protection.

Julia knew she was a mess and tried to cover herself with her hands, but he caught her wrists. "You are beautiful, but let's find a shower."

"And then what?" She sat up with his help and hopped off the table.

"My four-poster bed." He laughed at her look of alarm. "Yes, those stories about the bed are true. And yes, I think you want to try it, don't you?"

An involuntary shiver ran through her and he laughed again, cupping her elbow. "Come upstairs, *meu bem,* and you can see for yourself."

"Just a second. I didn't get to ask you last night, but where did you get the protection? Do you keep some here?" She fought to keep the jealousy out of her voice.

"These came from the safe upstairs."

She started to laugh and he gave her a mock-wounded look. "Do you think I want my family to have access to everything I own? They're nosy enough as it is." He struck a pose. "The Duke of Santas Aguas demands his privacy. Not that I get much," he admitted.

"As long as they haven't expired." But who else came here to meet Frank?

He read her mind. "I brought them over last year when it seemed like I would bring a guest to visit. But it didn't work out and she never was invited." He shrugged. "Our island is a very special place and she wasn't the right one."

Did he mean "our island" as in his family's island or as in Julia and Frank's island? She didn't have the nerve to ask.

"But you are the right one. The only one I have brought here."

"Really?"

"I swear. You fit here perfectly and you fit me perfectly, dripping with honey and your own juices…" His voice trailed off and she noted in surprise that his cock was stiffening again. He'd always been extremely eager before, but she assumed it was because he'd been barely twenty. How nice that hadn't changed.

"Take me upstairs, Franco. I'm feeling very naughty." Her voice was unusually husky and seductive. "Show me how the Duke of Santas Aguas disciplines a naughty woman."

He swept her up into his arms before her next breath. "How naughty have you been?"

"Very," she assured him.

"Good." He headed for the stairs and she couldn't stop giggling. Naughty didn't even begin to cover what she had in mind.

8

Fashionista Magazine: The Royal Review:

AS MUCH AS WE LOVE OUR own celebrity blogger
Countess Lily de Brissard, she's being stubbornly
hush-hush about certain royal wedding details, in-
cluding where the royal couple will honeymoon.
Although we admire her loyalty, we're forced to
speculate on the location. Some rumors say they'll
jet off to the Caribbean or the Riviera, and some
say they'll set sail on the Royal Vinciguerran
yacht through the Greek Isles.

One intriguing possibility is a stay on an exclusive private property, like the de Brissard
lavender farm, the groom's family chalet in the
Bavarian Alps or even the extensive Portuguese
ranch owned by Duke Francisco Duarte das Santas
Aguas. Far away from the clubs, nightlife (and
cameras), but of course most honeymooners are *so*
tired and would rather turn in to bed early… Check
back for more news from the only royal wedding
site with an inside source—*The Royal Review!*

FRANK LEFT JULIA ASLEEP IN the pink-and-still-red bedroom and walked out on the stone balcony in a pair of
shorts. He couldn't concentrate on his thoughts if he
saw her in that four-poster bed, remembering how she
had let him dominate her all day and most of the night.
By the end of the night, they'd stopped using protection
since both of them were healthy and she was on birth
control for her cycle.

He groaned at the memory of her hot, wet body surrounding him and forced himself to take a deep breath.
She brought out all the machismo and male power running through his veins that he thought was dampened
by modern society and time. The urge to plant his seed
and watch it grow.

He stared out over the sea. He loved the early morning on Belas Aguas—and the waters lived up to their
name of beauty, blue and sparkling in the eastern light.
He was a man of contradictions, tied to his land in Portugal by seven hundred years of blood and sweat. But
the sea was in his veins as well, thanks to a previous
Duke of Santas Aguas who sailed west to claim a lonely
green island in the middle of the ocean.

He had abandoned the sea since Julia had abandoned
him. He froze. She hadn't really abandoned him, he'd
realized that after getting his head shrunk by the university counselor. But maybe deep down, he still felt
that way. His brain knew that they had been very young
and odds were against their relationship succeeding, but
his heart wasn't nearly as smart.

He peeked in the bedroom, almost to make sure she
was still there. His phone sat on a table near the balcony door, and he picked it up, suddenly needing to

talk to someone about his amazing situation. He called George's private line.

"Hey, Frank! How are you? How are the renovations going?" George asked cheerfully.

Frank cringed guiltily. His time had been spent in more pleasurable activities than priming and painting walls—and boy, did those walls need it. "We bought the supplies and are starting to paint soon." As soon as Julia picked out colors. But that meant they had to leave the island and go to the hardware store on São Miguel.

"And how is Benedito?"

Frank exhaled. "He's fine, but he went back to the mainland when his wife was having some health problems." He reassured George's noises of concern. "No, nothing serious, as far as I understand."

"I am glad." George chuckled. "Quite a character, that man."

"Don't I know it."

"But you are doing the work alone? Or do you have help now?"

"Julia is staying here with me."

There was a long pause. "Then your meeting again is going well?" His worry was evident.

"Very well." Frank couldn't keep the satisfaction out of his voice. "She and I are working on the house."

"Really." His tone was dry. "Getting much work done?"

"George…" Frank choked back a snort.

His friend sighed. "None of my business, I know."

"If you're worried about the villa being ready, please don't. I have a crew of men coming from São Miguel to do the heavy tasks—"

"Frank, the villa is the least of my concerns. *You* are worrying me more than the out-of-date paint colors."

"They are pretty bad. I'll email you a photo of what Benedito did before he left."

George made an impatient noise. "Enough with the remodeling! I swear, between your interest in planning Stefania's wedding and redoing the villa, I was beginning to worry about your machismo."

Frank laughed. "Don't worry about *that*."

"But now I am worrying the other way! Are you sure you know what you are doing?"

"Did you know what you were doing when you invited Renata to Italy the same night you met her?" he retorted.

"Of course not! That is why I worry."

"Stop worrying! You've hovered over me like an old woman for years."

"I am not hovering over you like an old woman," George protested.

"Okay, like a mother hen. Cluck, cluck, cluck."

George's gasp of outrage did sound rather like a chicken. "Frank!"

"George!" he mimicked.

They both fell silent and then started to laugh at the ridiculous exchange.

"Ah, Frank, I do tend to fuss over people, don't I? Stevie and my grandmother will testify to that."

"And once upon a time, I did need you to look after me. But that was a long time ago."

"I know." George sighed. "So, you and Julia," he continued cheerfully. "An island vacation in your lovely villa."

"I promise, it will be beautiful for Stevie and her husband," Frank said hastily.

"Huh, we both know how little time they will take to appreciate their surroundings. But the privacy for them will be priceless. Between Stevie's royalty and Dieter's football fame, they will have few opportunities to be alone. I must thank you for that."

"You're most welcome. Have you talked with Jack lately? I received a couple texts from him, but he has been busy with his farm and managing the lavender perfume sales for Stevie's charity."

"The sales are going very well, Frank. Stevie will have more money to save the world, one woman and child at a time."

Frank smiled. "We're lucky to have her. And Dieter is a lucky man."

"And he better realize that," George growled.

"Or else we'll convene a multinational task force to convince him of the error of his ways."

"Count me in."

"Good." They both laughed, knowing they weren't kidding.

Frank was so tuned in to Julia, he could tell when she stirred in the bedroom behind him. "I have to go start the coffeepot now, George."

"Have a good time, Frank. Keep me posted. About you, not the villa," he clarified.

"And you, too." They said goodbye and Frank stepped back into the bedroom.

Julia rolled over and gave him a sleepy smile. "Sunny day?"

He grinned at her, his chest as warm as if the sun had risen inside him. "With you, every day is sunny."

JULIA FLIPPED THE LAST pancake onto her plate and sat down across from Frank at the kitchen island.

"This is such a treat for me, Julia. I can't tell you how much I miss American food sometimes." Frank was eating his third pancake along with *chouriço* and fresh fruit.

Julia suppressed a smile. Portuguese sausage on the side and local honey on top weren't typically American additions, but she was happy to cook for him, happy to have an appetite. Just happy to share a life with him.

Breakfast. Share a breakfast with him. She shook her head and poured some honey onto her pancake.

"What would you like to do today, Julia? We could go to the beach or hang out next to the pool."

She wiggled her fork at him. "Those walls aren't going to get painted on their own."

"We have a couple more days before I need to get the workmen from São Miguel."

Julia shook her head. "Frank, I thought you had a long list of items to fix on your to-do list for Stefania's honeymoon. We can't spend the whole time in bed."

"We can't?" He gave her a disappointed look.

It did sound wonderful, but she drew on her deep-seated sense of responsibility. "No, we can't. Not unless you want Stefania and Dieter to have a red-and-pink cabbage-rose bedroom and leaky faucet."

He lifted a black brow. "Stefania and Dieter are madly in love, will be newly married and alone for the first time in several weeks. I don't think they will be worrying about ugly bedspreads and plumbing deficiencies."

Julia shook her head. "But doesn't she deserve a beautifully romantic hideaway?"

He crumbled, just like she knew he would. He loved Stefania as much as one of his own sisters. "Of course." He stood and pulled her into his arms. "I just hate to have the island overrun with workmen yet." He nuzzled her neck.

She tipped her head to the side to allow him easier access. "Then we'll do some of it ourselves."

"Ourselves?" He looked skeptical, as if she meant "himself" while she stood around being decoratively useless.

"Yes, ourselves. My condo in Boston was a wreck when I bought it and I was the one who did most of the rehab. My dad did the electrical, but taught me to do the plumbing. After that, painting and carpentry work was a breeze."

"Really?"

"I'm a handy girl."

"And I'm a handy man." He demonstrated that by sliding his hands down to squeeze her bottom. She wore thin knit exercise shorts and his hand was hot on her skin.

She giggled. "Very handy indeed. But what do you say, Frank? Let's fix the place up together, and then you can bring over the workers for the bigger projects."

"You're going to be a distraction."

"A bad one?" She wiggled against him.

He nibbled her earlobe. "What do you think?"

"A good distraction. But rolling around in bed won't get the renovations done. If we don't do anything, we'll have to get outside help that much sooner, and that means losing our privacy."

He frowned at that idea. She knew privacy was a rare gift for him, being surrounded most of the time by family and staff at home. "Okay, Julia. We can do most of the work and delay bringing in the cleaning and landscaping staff for several more days."

"Great." She looked around. "Where should we start?"

He sighed, his warm breath tickling her. "The bathrooms. Paint, plumbing, the whole works. All the supplies are out in the storage shed." He reluctantly let go of her and drank the rest of his coffee. "Take your time with your breakfast—it'll take me a few minutes to carry the new materials in."

He trudged toward the door in mock disappointment but was whistling cheerfully by the time he went outside. He was such an active man and thrived on difficult, physical work. Julia quickly loaded the dishes into the dishwasher and headed upstairs. She had bragged about her do-it-yourself skills and it was time to prove it.

Julia eyed the master bathroom's ancient faucet with two faceted plastic knobs designed to look like crystals. A steady drip of water plopped into the sink.

Frank appeared in the doorway. "Lovely, isn't it?"

"Is this the same sink from the last time I was here?"

"Yep." He grunted as he set down a big cardboard box that held a new vanity cabinet. He straightened up and massaged his lower back. "I'm sure it is. We haven't fixed up the villa for years."

She opened the doors under the old sink and shut off the water, disconnecting the plastic trap and letting the water drain into a bucket. Frank carried a wrench and screwdriver into the bathroom and stopped when he saw her progress.

"Screwdriver." She held out her hand and he placed

it in her palm. She tried to undo the screws holding the cabinet to the wall, but they were too tight for her. She struggled for a minute and Frank knelt beside her.

"Here, let me."

She fought with the screws but he made an impatient noise and covered her hand with his. "You don't have to do this all by yourself."

"I'm used to it." She didn't mean it as a slam on him but his lips tightened.

They tussled briefly over the tool but he prevailed and quickly freed the vanity from the wall. His muscles bulged as he pulled it into the bedroom.

While he was taking the old fixture downstairs, Julia cut open the new box and had the new vanity and sink pushed up against the wall. It was a dark mahogany with a cream stone top and she found a new brushed nickel faucet in a nearby box.

"Julia!" he said in annoyance, his arms crossed over his chest.

"What?"

"That cabinet and sink are very heavy, and you are still getting over your injuries. I am not going to let you help with this renovation if you insist on doing everything by yourself."

She huffed out a breath. "I'm perfectly capable of doing work like this without straining myself."

"I mean it, Julia." His face hardened into what she privately called his "duke expression." She'd only seen it a few times. "If you don't leave the heavy lifting to me, I'll do all the work myself."

"And what would I do?"

"Sit on the terrace and enjoy the ocean view. Or else I'll take you back to São Miguel."

"You'd separate us for this?"

"For the sake of your health I would do anything."

"Oh." She hated to admit he was right. Although she'd been in excellent shape before her injury, she wasn't back up to her full strength and was starting to feel a bit of strain in her arms and shoulders.

"What is the American phrase? You can be the brain and I can be the brawn." He gave her a teasing smile.

"Oh, Frank." She pushed at him and he hugged her. He certainly was strong, built like an ox.

"We make a good team, you and I." He dipped his head to kiss her, and she threaded her fingers through his sleek black waves.

He reached under her shorts, inhaling sharply when he realized she wasn't wearing any underwear. His fingers found her damp core, opening her and playing with her hard little clit, teasing until it swelled. She widened her stance and spread her arms for balance on the sink top.

"You want me to take you like this?" His hands caressed and molded her bottom cheeks.

She couldn't speak, only nodded.

"God, Julia, you turn me into an animal." He nudged her knees even wider with his and pushed the fabric to the side. Somehow the band of fabric made her feel even more naked than if she had been totally bare. He gripped her hips and thrust into her, letting out a groan as he settled himself to the hilt.

"Move," she moaned, when it seemed as if he was determined to drive her crazy and stay still.

He pistoned in and out of her, shoving his hands under her tank top to cup her breasts. His big fingers rolled her nipples into diamond hard points, sending jolts of lust triangulating down to her clit.

She tossed her head back and he bit her earlobe. "Touch yourself, Julia. Rub your clit for me."

She did as he commanded and looked into the mirror above the sink. She gasped. Her eyes were dilated and hazy, her hair a wild tangle.

Frank caught her gaze in the mirror. "Look how sexy you are. I can't even leave you long enough to undress you."

They both appeared dressed, but it was obvious that he was possessing her body. And possessing her mind and heart, as well.

9

JULIA STOOD UP AND SET DOWN the paint roller, noting the smears on her fingers. The downstairs bathroom was mercifully a sandy taupe color now, covering Benedito's unfortunate experiments in interior design. Along with Julia's help, Frank had ordered sets of pretty aqua and off-white towels and rugs as well as some pale blue-green bottles made of bubbly glass. Although Frank was a typical guy and not interested in scented candles, she'd also convinced him to order several creamy vanilla pillar candles of varying heights and widths. He could understand the need for emergency lighting, but explaining tea-lights to him just resulted in incredulity that anyone would want such a useless, tiny candle.

The vanity was a rich, dark mahogany with a marble top, solid marble, not laminated to look like marble, or even cultured marble. Frank had mentioned casually that the quarry in Italy had sent him pictures of various slabs until he saw one that he liked.

Julia could see why he liked it. It probably would have made a nice statue for some church somewhere, because the stone was almost flawless, a beautiful creamy color that would look wonderful for years.

She decided not to wash the paint off her hands and brushes in the zillion-dollar sink and went into the kitchen.

Frank was doing the same, washing grime off his hands. She nudged him aside playfully, dunking her hands under the running water. He dumped soap on her and started scrubbing her hands with his.

His hands were such a contrast to hers—dark and tough, but with a gentle touch. Her hands were pale with long fingers, well-suited to stitching up lacerations and inserting IV lines into patients. Once, she even got to deliver a baby—not by choice, of course, since the mother had been in her car in the emergency room driveway. The paperwork afterward had been horrendous, but she got a secret thrill from seeing her name on the baby's birth certificate.

"I delivered a baby once," she blurted.

"You did?" His hands tightened for a second on hers. "Whose?"

"A patient who was having her fifth baby. They got caught at a train crossing and by the time they pulled into the emergency room driveway, the baby was coming. All the docs were tied up so I pulled on my gloves as I ran and got there just in time."

"That's amazing, Julia. You must have been so proud." He dried his hands and gave her the towel.

"It was special." She sighed, hanging up the towel on a hook near the stove. "Maybe I should have been a midwife. It's a happier profession than patching up sick and injured people all the time." But she knew why she hadn't gone into midwifery—for several years after

breaking up with Frank, she had a hard time looking
at babies without imagining a dark-haired, dark-eyed
laughing baby that looked suspiciously like him. Now
that she was thirty and her biological clock had started
making ominous noises, she didn't think that situation
would change any.

"You could always retrain for a different specialty or
get a different job. The emergency room sounds almost
as dangerous for the staff as it is for the patients."

He didn't know the half of it, but she shook her head
and pulled a couple of bottles of orange soda from the
fridge, giving one to Frank. It had a distinctly different taste than American orange sodas, more tangy like
real oranges. "I've never spent much time around babies
aside from my training."

He thanked her for the soda and took a deep drink.
"That hits the spot. It's getting warm outdoors. As for
babies, right now I have five nieces and nephews, all
under six years old or so. Two of my sisters married
right out of university and have been having babies
every year, it seems." He smiled fondly. "They are quite
adorable, and besides, it takes my mother's attention off
me, at least temporarily."

Because his mother wanted him to settle down and
have a baby? Of course she did. Frank was the only son
of a family that relied on the ancient custom of primo-
geniture—where the oldest son inherited everything.
He would need a son of his own to keep up the tradition and not splinter the family holdings. Now that he
had passed his thirtieth birthday, maybe his biological
clock was ticking, too.

But she didn't ask. She was afraid to bring up the
question, afraid to hear the answer. For all she knew,

his mother had picked out a suitable upper-class Portuguese maiden for a potential bride. Maybe she was even a virgin. Was that a requirement to marry a duke? Virginity—at least for the women—had been a requirement to marry into royalty for hundreds of years, petering out only in the last couple decades.

Curiosity overcame her. It wasn't as if she were still a virgin, although that was in fact his fault in the first place. If he hadn't been so darn sexy at twenty and she hadn't been so crazy about him...well, as the saying went, the more things changed, the more they stayed the same. She'd eagerly participated in the Azorean version of the *droit de seigneur,* the largely legendary custom of the lord of the manor to get first dibs at the local virgins. "Are you seeing anyone at home?"

He looked shocked and then guilty. Guilty?

"Frank, did you forget to mention something? Or someone?"

"Julia, it is not what you think."

Her stomach knotted, the orange soda suddenly making her queasy. She forced herself to speak calmly. "Why don't you tell me what is going on?" After all, she didn't have any claim on him—not anymore.

He set his bottle down on the counter. "My sister has a friend—her name is Paulinha and we've known each other for years." He sighed. "Paulinha has never made it much of a secret that she considers me more than a brotherly figure. But me, I didn't feel the same. On the other hand, I always thought that I would be married with a family by now. Paulinha is a soft-spoken woman, shy and good-natured."

Julia blinked her eyes hard. Her own escapades at work would definitely not qualify as soft-spoken and shy. Although she was fairly good-natured, wasn't she? Maybe not, especially to the crazy patient who'd cracked her in the head. But that was his fault, not hers, and she tried not to feel guilty for getting herself out of that mess.

Undoubtedly Princess Paulinha would have screamed or swooned like a proper upper-class Portuguese *senhorinha*. Julia had swooned, sure, but she had the concussion to blame. Even then it was only a temporary swoon before she'd done what she had to do.

"And you see Paulinha as a possibility in the marriage and family department?" Julia fiddled with the soda label, peeling the corner down with her thumbnail. Was it weird or what, discussing eligible women with the man she'd desperately loved so many years ago? How sophisticated they both were.

"No." His reply was short and immediate. "Not anymore. I was considering spending more time with her to find out if there could be sparks between us, but the ever-practical Benedito pointed out that I was fifteen hundred kilometers away from her and it didn't seem to bother me."

"And Benedito could tell you weren't pining away for her?" she asked skeptically.

"Oh, yes. Benedito knows pining when he sees it." He gave her a crooked smile. "His rural yokel facade hides a master observer of human nature. Besides, he has known me since I was a baby."

"Did you pine for me, Frank?" Was that why Benedito had practically shoved them together at the farmer's market?

"What do you think?" He set his bottle down on the

counter with a harsh clink. "I never wanted you to go in the first place."

She bit her lip. "And I missed you, too."

"We were both young and stupid," he said bluntly. "I try to think that everything happened for a reason, but it was difficult for me for a long time."

"But now we're both here and having a good time together, right?" Emotions from the past and present were threatening to overwhelm her, so she strove for a light, happy tone.

"Right. A good time," Frank echoed, a faraway look in his eyes. He gave a quick shake of his head and came back to the present. "Speaking of a good time, I made plans for us to go to São Miguel for the day. The bathrooms are both finished, so we deserve a break before tackling that red abomination in the bedroom."

"Great!" Julia could use a good distraction. Standing around painting and talking to Frank about heavy topics was bringing up more than she bargained for. "Let's get some groceries, as well. We're almost out of coffee."

He gasped. "No, not the last of the coffee! There's no way I can lift a paintbrush without my caffeine."

"So running out of food is acceptable, but not coffee?"

"Exactly."

"A man after my own heart."

He finished the last of his soda and rinsed the bottle. "I am indeed."

Julia gave him a wary look, wondering if he meant that literally, as well.

"I can have the boat ready in ten minutes. Do you need to stop by your parents' apartment for anything?"

She nodded. "Water the plants, check the mail, that sort of thing." She had only been gone a few days, but her parents were relying on her to make sure their place was still in one piece.

"Sure. We'll get some lunch and then shop for groceries right before we come back." He kissed her lightly before striding out the door. God, he looked as good from the back as he did from the front.

Julia disposed of her own soda bottle, determined to stop agonizing and mooning over everything. She had agreed to stay with him on a temporary, spring-fling basis, not for deep heart-to-heart, soul-baring conversations.

Maybe it was the fact they were the only two people on his island, an island heavy with meaning and memories. A trip to cheerful, relatively crowded São Miguel would lighten her mood. It was difficult to keep her focus on the present—her heart wanted to go back to the past and her mind wouldn't stop thinking about the future.

FRANK EASILY DOCKED AND secured the boat at the marina on the island of São Miguel. He helped Julia down the ramp. "How is your head feeling today?"

She blinked. Come to think of it, her head had been fine the past several days. Maybe fantastic regular sex released some of those natural endorphin painkillers. "I'm doing really well, Frank. No problems."

"You sure?" He stared at her. "Because if you're feeling up for it, I thought we could take a side trip to one of the smaller villages here. You haven't seen much besides the main town here and my island, which doesn't have anything interesting to look at."

She squeezed his hand, letting her breast rub against his arm. "It has you."

"Well, that is…" He cleared his throat, a ruddy flush creeping under his olive skin. "Anyway, you have to tell me if it's too much for you."

"I'm a sturdy girl, Frank. I'll let you know if you're too much for me." She could tell he was about ready to pitch her back on the boat and return to their island, or at least far enough out to sea to have some privacy. But she tugged him along the dock to the sidewalk. Nothing wrong with a little anticipation. "Where to?"

"There." He pointed to the motorcycle rental shop next to the marina.

She grinned. "I haven't been on one of those in years. Can we get the blue one?"

"Sure." He rented the blue motorcycle along with a couple helmets and went over a quick safety lesson with the shop owner. Julia fastened the smaller helmet onto her head and Frank double-checked the strap. "No point in giving you another headache." He fastened a backpack to the rack behind her.

This probably wasn't what her doctor had in mind, but she didn't care and hopped behind Frank. He took off and she wrapped her arms around his waist.

After a couple minutes, she got used to leaning with him as he went around corners, holding on tight as he braked for the occasional pedestrian or farm animal. They were pretty much at the same pace. In fact, Julia thought she could jog faster than they were riding.

She pinched his hard stomach to get his attention and he jumped, turning his head slightly. "Are you okay? Do you want me to slow down?"

"No, Frank. Go faster."

"What?" He pulled up to a stop sign leading into a more rural, hilly area and flipped up his visor.

She flipped up hers as well so he could see her. "Look at me—I'm doing fine. I don't want to take a spill, but I'm not made of glass, either. It's a perfect day to be out here on a motorcycle—let's take advantage of it."

His white smile sparkled against his skin. "Get ready." He flipped down the visor and she did the same. Checking for cross-traffic, he gunned the machine along. Finally, the wind was whipping past her face, the air clear and fresh as it rolled in from the Atlantic. The road curved and dipped through green hills and rocky black soil. She spotted small settlements with low-slung white houses, sheep and cattle dotting the hills to graze.

She settled her cheek on Frank's back and sighed in happiness, her cares and worries flying away like unsecured cargo. And good riddance. She didn't want any of them back, especially those heavy memories that gripped her mind as the headaches had gripped her skull.

He patted her hand resting on his middle, as if he picked up on her thoughts. He was so sweet. He'd always been that way, even when his sweetness—and stubbornness—had caused their previous breakup. Of course it couldn't have been her own legendary stubbornness that contributed to it, not at all. Her motto back then should have been *My way, or the highway.*

She'd just been scared and upset. Instead of choosing to cling to him during their rough times, she'd shoved him away. Even after returning to the States, she thought about calling him a hundred times, a thousand times. He would have been easy to find at the university, and maybe they could have patched their relationship back together. She could have called his estate in Portugal and passed along a message. But she hadn't—and neither had he. Why was that? Was he as scared as she was? It was hard to imagine strong, brawny Frank being afraid of anything. She wanted to ask him but couldn't shout such a deep question like that as they rocketed along the highway.

She'd had over a decade to think and had come to the conclusion that the highway was no fun unless you had someone riding along with you. Like today.

Julia hugged him and kissed his shoulder. He straightened in surprise and the bike bobbled a second. "Stop distracting me," he turned his head to shout. "Or I'll crawl along at twenty kilometers per hour."

"Fine," she shouted back, hiding her smile in his back. "I want to go faster than that cow I just saw."

He picked up the speed again, and the ocean breeze began to take on a peculiar smell as they went around a corner, the vista opening onto a larger town nestled between a mountain and the ocean. The view was beautiful, but the air had sort of a sulfuric, rotten-eggs smell. Rather interesting combination, the whole fire-and-brimstone smell coming from a picturesque village.

The wind changed and blew away the eggs-gone-bad odor. Frank eased off the throttle as they approached the town. She was glad this time because she could see the houses and people better.

"This is Furnas," he announced, unstrapping his helmet and helping her do the same.

"Furnace? Is that why it smells like that?" Her hair immediately sprang into its normal fluff. Not even the heavy helmet could make it behave. She shook it and fingercombed it down anyway.

"Spelled a little different in Portuguese, but the same idea. That," he said, pointing at the mountain ahead of them, "is an active volcano."

She was taken aback as she gazed up at the rounded mountain. Visions of rivers of lava and clouds of ash raining down as innocent Azorean islanders fled with screams of terror came to mind. Although on an island, there was only so far you could flee before you got to the ocean.

"Don't worry, the last big eruption of this volcano was in the 1600s."

"Isn't another overdue, then?" she asked.

"No, no," he assured her. "There are underwater eruptions quite frequently. They probably help vent the pressure here on dry land."

She rolled her eyes. Not the most reassuring geological theory she'd ever heard. Frank was a farmer and rancher, not a volcanologist. However, no ominous puffs of smoke were issuing from the top, and the local people were going about their daily lives, shopping and visiting without any particular look of panic.

"Come on, let's enjoy the town." He steadied the motorcycle as she climbed off, the pull of muscles in her inner thighs and butt making her walk bowlegged for a minute.

He watched her with an avid gleam in his eye and she shook her finger at him. "Behave yourself, you miscreant."

"Miscreant? How very strict and old-fashioned you sound. I like it." He wiggled his eyebrows.

She grabbed his shirtfront to pull him close. "Don't make me punish you, Franco."

His black gaze threw golden sparks. "What if I want you to?"

"No promises." She kissed him quickly but thoroughly, pushing him away at the end.

"The punishment starts," he groaned, lifting the backpack onto his shoulders.

Julia laughed and took his hand. "Hey, Frank, do you have any water in that backpack?" The trip had dried out her mouth.

"No, but we'll get some around the corner."

A minute later, Julia was looking at the Cro-Magnon version of a drinking fountain. "And people drink this?" she whispered, not wanting to offend anyone.

"Furnas is famous for its hot springs and spa waters. This spring is called *Agua Santa,* holy water." A spigot came out of a stone wall, the water spilling into an iron-stained basin below.

"Like your estate in Portugal."

He smiled down at her. "Yes, my land is named after a spring as well, but a cold artesian spring instead of a hot spring."

"I wonder which tastes better."

"You'll have to find out for yourself."

She blinked. This was the first time he'd mentioned visiting his family estate on the mainland—at least this time. Eleven years previously, he'd invited her there and discussed the land and people in great detail. They all seemed perfectly pleasant, but his duties outside of the estate were something different.

One event had been particularly frightening to her. Frank, having turned eighteen, had been invited to the

Spanish royal palace for a state dinner with the king
and queen of Spain. He of course thought nothing of
meeting royalty since he was pretty close to royalty
himself. He mentioned the king and queen fondly and
personally, if not by first name. It had stayed with her
ever since.

And, of course, his estate regularly hosted the aris-
tocracy and upper crust of Europe. Frank's mother, the
Dowager Duchess, enjoyed high-society life and threw
extended house parties at the huge manor house. Frank
had described the formal dinners with seven courses,
bottomless wineglasses and enough silverware to support a small nation. Julia could get through dinner without blowing her nose into her napkin or scratching her
scalp with a salad fork, but had to admit a real sense of
intimidation.

Oh, sure, she would have been a real hit hosting those
parties if she'd married Frank—the nineteen-year-old
college-drop-out duchess who couldn't even speak Portuguese.

She wondered if that had partially spooked her from
keeping up a relationship with him. "Have you seen the
king and queen of Spain recently?"

He gave her a puzzled look. "Not since the baptism
of one of their grandchildren a few years back. Why?"

"I was wondering if they'd ever tasted your spring
water. Maybe they could give it their royal seal of ap-
proval."

He shook his head and turned away—maybe in disappointment? She touched his arm in apology. "I'm
sorry, Frank. I didn't mean to be flip. The springs sound
really nice."

He smiled at her—all was forgiven. He paid a nearby

vendor for the loan of a pair of sturdy glasses. He handed her one. "You have to fill your own cup. Otherwise, it doesn't work as well."

"What is it supposed to do?" She bent and twisted open the faucet, an ominous-smelling liquid spilling into her cup.

He followed and did the same. "It does what you need it to do. If you are sick, it makes you well. If you are weak, it makes you strong. If you have a heavy burden, it lightens you."

Julia stared at the water. "That's a lot for a cup of water to do."

He swirled his around, almost up to the rim. "That's why they call it 'holy water.' Because it can perform miracles. What miracle do you want, Julia?"

Him. She wanted him. But she was still a mess, and he deserved someone who wasn't banged and bruised up, mentally and physically. "I would like for my headaches to go away for good."

His eyes darkened in concern. "They haven't been bothering you today, have they? Otherwise, I can call a cab to take us back to the boat."

"No, my head feels okay. I haven't really had a bad headache since the day we met at the farmer's market."

"That was a shock for me, too. But a good one," he hastily added. He lifted his glass. "To good surprises."

"And miracles." Julia clinked her rim against his. She took a deep breath and drank. "Aack!" she sputtered. The water lived up to its iron-colored promise, so rich with minerals that it almost had a gritty texture as it battled its way down her throat.

Frank drained his glass without a wince and even smacked his lips.

"Well, I won't need to worry about my iron intake for the day." She smacked her lips as well, mostly to get the taste off them. "Like medicine—it has to taste bad to work well."

"Good things come with a price." Frank took her glass and drank the rest of her water before handing both glasses back to the nearby vendor.

Wasn't that the truth. Unfortunately, she'd paid a high price for stupid things, too. "What's next?" she asked brightly, not wanting to dwell on the negative on such an interesting, if smelly, day.

Frank took her hand and they wandered through the town, the natives obviously very proud of literally living on the edge of the volcano. Little shops full of bottled spring water and T-shirts aimed for the tourist trade while the usual cafés, delis and bakeries were there for the local population. "Here we go." Frank stopped at a gate marked with a large sign written several times in various alarming fonts and colors.

"Hot danger?" she asked.

"Thank you." He wiggled his eyebrows at her. "I've never been called *that* before."

"Not you." She squeezed his hand and he spun her around so her back was against the iron fence.

"You don't think I'm hot and dangerous?" He ran his fingers up her arm next to the heavy curve of her breast. He brushed the side where no one could see, and her nipples hardened instantly against the cotton of her shirt. "I'll have to work harder to convince you of that." He swiveled his hips so his pants' zipper rested on her hip. Even through the thick fabric, she could practically feel every inch of him. Even at rest, so to speak, he was firm and long, ready to spring up at her slightest touch.

"I think you're very hot and dangerous." Her voice was breathy.

"Good." He leaned in, innocently kissing her cheek and then not-so-innocently flicking her earlobe with his tongue.

She let out a little moan and he pulled back, a gleam of satisfaction in his eyes. "But, unfortunately, we are only here to see the hot, dangerous springs."

"Fine." Her lips pulled into a little pout, but she couldn't very well go mauling Frank in public. He was a big fish in the small pond of the Azores, and everybody knew who he was. Many of them knew him personally, as well. She supposed he was expected to kiss women in public and generally show off his macho side—not that she minded. She loved being the recipient of a certain aspect of his macho side. And his sweet side. And even his grouchy side when the coffee was still brewing.

"Shall we go inside, *meu bem?*"

The endearment sent warm fuzzy feelings through her. "Let's see if the smell lives up to the hype."

They wandered through a setting that reminded her of a park—if a park had dirty brown boiling mud pits that looked as if some primordial monster was forming from the dangerous ooze. Occasionally large gunky bubbles would rise to the surface and then pop, wafting that lovely sulfur odor toward her. As a nurse, she was unfortunately reminded of certain rough evenings in the emergency department with patients who must have eaten a buffet of cabbage, broccoli and beans before arriving for care.

Fortunately, they turned a corner and came to clear, or rather clearer, water. Here the water probably had more of a calcium or salt content, because it left a crystal-white coating that looked like snow or icicles depending on where it dripped. A pool of water lay below the walkway they traveled, and Julia was careful to watch her step and stay well back from the railing.

An older woman with short black hair shot with gray sat nearby with husked corn on the cob and small brown potatoes in a basket on the path just past the walkway. Frank asked her a question in Portuguese and she replied, pointing at the water.

He grinned and handed her a few euros. "She says it's almost ready."

Julia knew what was coming when the woman hauled on a rope to pull up a steaming hot mesh bag from the spring itself. The vendor carefully drained most of the water and opened the bag into a battered metal colander. Cobs and potatoes tumbled out, and the woman tossed one of each into two rectangular carry-out trays. *"Bom appetito."*

"Thank you." They walked along the path for a few minutes. Julia blew on the golden corn cob and debated how to eat the potato without any utensils. The corn cooled faster, and she decided to try that first, nibbling along it.

Frank took a bite of his, as well. "Well, what do you think?" he asked, once they were done chewing.

"It does taste different—but not bad. Almost pre-salted." She ate another row, getting used to the different flavor. The corn grown here probably tasted different in the first place due to the volcanic soil, a huge contrast from the sandy and sometimes swampy Massachusetts ground.

He picked up his potato and bit into it like an apple.

"Needs butter," he mumbled, the unadorned root vegetable starch obviously a challenge for him.

"Want me to find some water for you to wash that down?" she asked sweetly, guessing that any taps here in the park were probably just as odiferous as the first one.

He gave her a sidelong glance that promised retribution later and finally swallowed. "No, thank you."

Julia laughed and finished her corn. It actually was quite flavorful and juicy. The spring probably cooked it quickly. Frank abandoned his potato and switched to the corn. She consented to taking a small bite of potato just for the flavor experience but he was right—it did need butter.

"Lunch will be much more flavorful, I promise." Frank took the paper trays and pitched the remnants into a garbage can.

"More of that chunky fish stew?" He had cooked that for her a few days ago, and it had been delicious.

"Not today." He took her hand. "Benedito's cousin lives nearby, and they are having us to lunch today for the local specialty—*cozido*."

"I've never heard of that dish."

He grinned as if holding a big secret. "It's very local. You can't find it anywhere else in the world."

Julia grimaced slightly. She was always leery of claims like that, especially on islands where truly odd bits of seafood or meat could be claimed as delicacies. "We're not eating cod brains or pig's private parts, are we?"

He roared in laughter. "If you've lived around the world like I have, you'd be worried, too," she retorted. "My father is a very adventurous eater and my mother is always hovering over him to make sure he hasn't caught some rare parasite."

He caught her hand and they walked along the path. The trees were green and lush, and she had the same disjointed feeling she'd always had in the Azores. Portuguese, but not Mediterranean. Atlantic seacoast, but not American. Tropical oranges, pineapples, even tea plantations, but not hot and sunny.

"My French friend Jack worked in all sorts of bad conditions, and he finally got sick last year. I had worried about that for years, but you can't tell a doctor anything."

She snickered in agreement, knowing many more doctors than Frank. "Is he okay now? What did he catch?"

"Dysentery."

"Oh." Julia groaned. She'd only seen a couple cases of that but knew it was a nasty, possibly fatal disease if not treated properly.

"He's okay now, but he needed several months to recover. In a fortunate twist of fate, he met Lily, an American travel writer, as he was traveling home to Provence. He was planning to sit in the sun to recuperate but instead wound up falling in love. He and Lily just got married last summer and now they are having a baby." His smile was heartfelt, but maybe a bit wistful.

"How exciting! Oh, look at that hot spring. The water looks almost silver." Julia hastily changed the subject. Frank came from a big family and probably still wanted lots of little Portuguese babies running around. A young, fertile wife in her early twenties would be the best for that. Funny to think that many women Julia's age spent their twenties trying to avoid pregnancy and their thirties chasing it.

"There is one pair of taps nearby that has two different springs. One tap has silvery residue and the other is iron." Frank seemed to shake off his tinge of melancholy and checked the time on his phone. "Almost time to get lunch. Let's hop on the bike and go up to the caldera."

"What's the caldera?" They went around a turn and Julia saw they were close to the entrance.

He winked. "The rim of the volcano."

10

Julia wasn't sure about going to the rim of any volcano, dormant or not, but a few minutes later, Frank stopped the motorcycle in a small parking lot above the town.

"There's a lake in the volcano." Julia had thought it would be a gaping crater. "It's beautiful." The water was a deep, dark blue, sparkling under the sun.

"I'm glad you like it. The volcano is cooking our lunch." He tugged her along.

"We're not roasting hot dogs over it, are we?"

"Much more fancy."

Around the corner was another moonscape of crusted white land. Apparently this was safe for walking, since a handful of elderly men stood around on it smoking cigarettes, as if the sulfur fumes weren't enough. Black mounds of dirt dotted the flat area like giant anthills.

One man spotted Frank and called out enthusiastically. Frank waved in response. "Come meet our chefs."

"Chefs?"

He tugged her along across the crunchy soil—almost as if they were walking on a frozen lake and she wasn't sure if it would hold them. And she could swear the soles of her shoes were getting hotter as they went.

Frank greeted the men and introduced her to them, remembering each of their first and last names, and with Portuguese names, that was several apiece. The men were clearly flattered at being remembered by the Duke of Santas Aguas and treated her as if she were a princess. Or a duchess.

"A pleasure, *senhorina*." One man—she thought his name was José—gave her a little bow and gestured at the black mound closest to them. "We bring food out here at five o'clock this morning."

A couple men busied themselves with a shovel, clearing the dirt away to reveal a pail with a lid. Another man hooked a hoe into the lid handle and lifted what looked like a five-gallon metal bucket.

"Here's our lunch."

"Oh, um, are we picnicking here?" Julia looked around for somewhere to sit. She couldn't even smell what lunch might be.

Frank translated her question and the men laughed good-naturedly. "José says if he sits on the ground he is not getting back up again," Frank told her, pointing at José who clutched comically at his back and limped for a few steps. "No, we are going to his house to eat with him and his family."

The men wrapped the pail in a couple of old horse blankets and Frank helped lug it to the parking lot. He pretended to lift it onto the back of the motorcycle as if to drive it to José's house and the old men laughed again. The Duke of Santas Aguas was obviously a well-admired young man.

The pail made it safely into a compact car's backseat,

and the caravan of cars and motorcycle wound down the hill to a pretty white-washed two-story house. José honked the horn to announce that the ducal procession had arrived, and an older woman came out the front door, wiping her hands on a dishtowel. She wore glasses and had short, reddish-brown hair that puffed slightly around her face.

From the way she gestured and scolded José, Julia guessed that she was his wife. The men bore the pail into the house under her strict supervision, and then she turned to Frank. "Your Grace. Welcome to our home." She even curtsied a bit. It was the first time Julia'd seen anyone treat Frank so formally, and it reminded her that he was indeed a powerful nobleman, cousin to Portuguese royalty, and accustomed to much finer things in life than she was.

Frank bowed back and took the woman's hand in greeting. "It is our honor to be here, *Senhora* Magdalena." He introduced her to Julia, holding the older lady's hand the whole time.

"Please come in, Your Grace, *Senhorina* Julia." Magdalena gestured toward the back of the house. "I must make sure the men are not ruining our lunch."

"Of course. What would we men do without the ladies to watch over us?"

Magdalena gave a surprisingly young-sounding giggle at Frank's gallantry. He furthered his reputation as a gentleman by tucking Magdalena's hand into his left elbow and reaching for Julia's for his right side.

The three of them entered the house. The living room was small but stuffed with comfortable-looking furniture, and the dark wood dining room table was set with what had to be the good china, white with pink pastel roses around the rims.

José poked his head out of the kitchen. "Hey, Don Franco, you already got a pretty girl, leave mine alone!"

"José!" Magdalena hissed, mortified at her husband's lack of respect for their noble guest. She let go of Frank's arm and burst into a torrent of Portuguese, waving her dishtowel at her husband's head.

The older man just laughed and ducked, obviously used to baiting his wife. She chased him into the kitchen and appeared a moment later, smoothing her ruffled dignity with a serene smile. "Would you like to see the opening of the *cozido?*"

"I'd love to," answered Julia. She might need an extra few minutes to bolster her courage for eating their mystery-meat lunch.

The kitchen was a smaller version of the one in Frank's villa, dark wood and tiled walls. The pail sat on the center island, surrounded by more women— probably the wives of the men she'd met up at the caldera. The men leaned against the countertops, joking with each other. José put on oven mitts and popped the lid. They all sighed in pleasure as a delicious scent immediately filled the room.

Julia breathed out a sigh of relief, as well. Pork, if she wasn't mistaken. She could handle that. Magdalena reached into the pail with tongs and started pulling out tender chunks of meat, wedges of cabbage, potatoes and other vegetables and plump brown loops of sausage.

Julia's mouth watered. "So the pail acts as a slow cooker and the volcano supplies the heat?"

Frank nodded. "And it's first come, first served to the hot pits where you bury the food. That's why José got there at five this morning to make sure he got a good spot."

"All that work for us?"

José overheard her question. "No work, just an honor. The Duke, he is very good to our little islands."

Magdalena chipped in, "He paid for the school playground, new roof for the church, bus for the handicapped children, new machines at the hospital—"

Frank waved his hands. "Please, please, you're embarrassing me." His cheeks were turning ruddy, and Julia smiled.

She decided to take the focus off Frank to let him recover from the shower of well-deserved praise. "Magdalena, you speak very good English." Julia carried a platter of *cozido* to the table and set it where the older woman indicated.

"She should," said José, pouring a rich red wine into the goblets. "We lived in Falls River, Massachusetts, for thirty years. They say Falls River is the eighth island of the Azores since so many of us moved there when we were young." The other men nodded.

Magdalena shooed everyone into a chair. She and José sat at the head and foot of the table. Julia sat between José and Frank and the other couples filled in to make about fourteen people at the table.

Julia smiled at their host. "Of course, Falls River." It was a heavily Azorean enclave famous for its good food and rich culture. "I live in Boston now, but my parents retired back here. We lived here briefly when I was young—on the Air Force base."

"Eh, we all move back and forth between Massachusetts and the Azores. If you lived here when you were a kid, you already an Azorean, right?"

"Well..." She'd need to learn Portuguese much better to get away with that claim. "That's kind of you to say."

"Just the truth." José tapped his wineglass. "A toast." The table obediently quieted. "A toast to Don Franco, Duke of Santas Aguas, who grew into a fine man like his father and grandfather before him. They would be proud."

Frank blinked in emotion, but José wasn't done yet. "And to the lovely *Senhorina* Julia, an Azorean-American beauty. Welcome home!"

It was Julia's turn to blush, and she gave what she hoped was a gracious nod to the cheers and claps. She sipped at her wine and filled her plate with juicy pork chunks, sausage and fork-tender cabbages and potatoes. The conversation dimmed as they ate their lunch, but grew in volume as the wine flowed and the eating slowed. It was a mix of English on her behalf and fast Azorean Portuguese. Weather, politics, the local economy were all hot topics that brought out fervent gestures and much fork-pointing.

During one particularly vigorous argument, Julia leaned over to Frank. "I didn't know you were such a philanthropist."

He grimaced. "I tried to stay anonymous, but Benedito likes to brag about me. He and his wife have three daughters, so I'm the closest thing he has to a son."

"But that's so sweet."

"No, you are." He caught her hand under the table and squeezed. She squeezed back and he smiled at her, his eyes like melted chocolate.

No, Frank was sweet. Sweet to her, his friends, their hosts who respected him for being a decent man more than just a duke. Nobility was an accident of birth, but good character was no accident.

She realized they had been staring into each other's eyes for quite a while when the table quieted. She and Frank broke eye contact and Julia stared at her plate, her cheeks hot.

Conversation quickly picked up, but Julia caught a twinkle in José's eye and quickly hidden smiles from the women.

Goo-goo eyes and holding hands at a table full of doting Azoreans—phone lines would be burning hotter than the volcano ten seconds after they left.

Frank gave her hand one last squeeze and picked up his wine glass. "I would like to propose a toast to our host José and his lovely wife Magdalena for inviting us into their home, and to all of you as well for welcoming Julia and me to Furnas. *Saude!* Cheers!"

His sentiments were echoed amidst the clink of goblets. Madgalena brought out a huge American-style chocolate cake and traditional pastries. Julia had to decline a second dessert. "I don't want to tip over the motorcycle."

"A little girl like you," Madgalena scoffed, clearing away a plate. "Me, on the other hand…" She patted her well-rounded hip.

José grabbed her around the waist. "More of you to love, *meu bem*. And there are other things to ride." He wiggled his bushy salt-and-pepper eyebrows.

"Oh, you!" She swatted at him with her dishtowel, blushing fiercely.

"What? Like a bicycle. Or a car. Or a donkey."

"I'll give you a donkey!" Magdalena gave him one

last smack with the towel before flouncing off to the kitchen, José's uproarious laughter in her wake.

Julia smiled at their comfortable relationship, much like her parents. Maybe that was why she'd never gotten terribly serious about any of the men she'd dated. They had been pleasant men but she'd never felt truly at ease with them. She hadn't been able to imagine herself years in the future, older and plumper, pouring wine, setting out a nice dinner for them and their friends.

She offered to help in the kitchen but was roundly rebuffed for being a guest. Frank chatted with the men for a while, but then stood and made his goodbyes, reminding Julia they still had to run their errands and get back to Belas Aguas before dark.

They put on their jackets and helmets and rode away with a roar, waving goodbye until they turned the corner.

The earlier haze had burned off and the mountains were even greener as they rode along, reminding her of photos of Hawaii with its rich volcanic soil.

Frank was warm and solid in her arms, and she wished they were back on the boat so she could hold him face-to-face. As they got farther away from Furnas, she could swear that he was hitting bumps on purpose. Every time he hit a bumpy spot, the throbbing between her thighs increased, and her hands tightened on him. Once they got back to the boat, she would free him from his pants and take him inside her, make him relieve her aching desire.

He found a spot in the road that probably hadn't been paved since her first trip to the Azores and she let out a moan. The road, the throbbing of the engine, the sly touches and teasing...

Frank unexpectedly slowed and pulled into a narrow country lane. He drove the bike under a canopy of hanging trees and shut off the engine. The sound of the countryside gradually returned to her ears as they adjusted to the sudden silence.

He swiveled on the bike and flipped up his visor. "Julia, are you in pain? I didn't realize this road was in such poor condition."

"No, Frank, I'm fine." She fought to bring her breathing under control and waved a hand.

He didn't believe her. "Let me see your face." He popped off her helmet. "You're all flushed, and your eyes are hazy."

"I'm fine." She just wanted to get back to the boat and have her wicked way with him.

A devilish smile spread across her face and he unzipped her jacket. "Your nipples are hard, Julia." He ran his palm over each breast. "And if I were to touch here, would you be wet?" He slipped his fingers along the center seam of her jeans. "Soaking wet. I think our bumpy ride turned you on."

Her face flushed even hotter. "Get me to the boat and you'll find out."

"No, I think I'll find out here." He unbuttoned her shirt and flipped open the front clasp of her bra. The cool woodsy air tightened her nipples into hard little buds.

"Frank." She half gasped, half moaned at the sensation of the breeze on her bare skin. "What if someone comes?"

He backed her up so she rested against a big tree. "I hope more than one person comes," he joked, bending to take her into his mouth, and then all joking was finished. His mouth was hot and wet, like a mineral spring bubbling around her. He licked and nibbled at each swollen tip. She cried out and clutched his head with one hand and the tree with another.

He chuckled and slid his hand between her legs, rubbing at the damp fabric, pressing the thick seam up into her throbbing flesh. Shockingly, she started to climax from just that stimulation in addition to the bike's vibration. She tried to fight it, wanted to wait, but he rubbed harder and sucked her breast deep, pinching the other nipple as she came. Her head fell back and she moaned in pleasure.

He finally slowed and looked up at her. "God, you're beautiful. And so sexy. I bet you were almost ready to come on that bike, weren't you?"

She nodded, her face red with embarrassment and desire. Despite her climax, she was still wound up, still on edge.

He stood, his jeans bulging in the front. "And you're ready to come again, aren't you?"

"Frank." His name came out in a strangled groan, and he laughed.

"How would you like it this time, Julia?" He rested his hands on either side of her face. "Do you want me to take you against the tree? Or do you want me to lie down so you can ride me like the bike? You pick."

"But Frank, are you sure we're alone out here?"

He stopped and listened. The birdsong had returned after the noise of the engine disappeared, and there were no other sounds to indicate company. "Nobody but us." He kissed her, cupping her breast until she arched against his palm. "Tell me, sweet Julia—the tree, or like the motorcycle?"

"The bike." She blushed again. It was dangerous and naughty to do this, not too far off the road. But, oh, was it sexy.

"Good." He pulled a folded picnic blanket off the back of the motorcycle and spread it on the ground. Her legs were still wobbly, so she waited for him to return. She kicked off her shoes and he undid her jeans, pulling them off but leaving her tiny black satin panties on.

Julia took off the heavy jacket and her blouse and bra, setting them aside. Frank picked up the jacket. "Wear this."

She slipped into the jacket and started to zip it, but he stopped her. "Leave it open. I want to see your pretty white tits against the black leather. If you're a good girl, you can ride back to the boat like that, your nipples rubbing the leather."

Her knees almost buckled again and he gave her a wicked smirk. His jeans came off quickly and she saw how he strained against his briefs. She reached into the waistband and freed his hard cock as he groaned with relief. "That's it, Julia. I've been aching for you for hours."

She wrapped her fingers around him, marveling again at his length and heft. He was dark brown with ropy veins struggling along his shaft, his head a deep plum, engorged with blood. As she gently squeezed him, a silvery bead formed on the tip.

Impulsively, she dropped to her knees on the picnic blanket and flicked the droplet with her tongue. He let out an agonized moan, his fingers digging into her scalp. "No, no, no. Oh, not that. I won't be able to—"

She cut off his words when her lips closed over him. He rocked back on his heels in shock as she sucked him hard. Up and down she bobbed her head, his salty taste coating her tongue and his musky scent filling her nostrils. She cupped his heavy sac with both hands and petted him, enjoying his gasps of pleasure. Her own secret places pulsed in time to his, her panties dampening as she got caught up in his pleasure.

He jerked inside her mouth and she thought for a second that he was going over the edge. Instead he held her head still. "Stop," he gritted out, pulling away from her. He lay down on the blanket and tugged her toward him.

She crawled up his body, her breasts swaying free from the jacket. His eyes widened in appreciation. "That is exactly what I had in mind." He brushed his thumbs over her nipples, and she nearly collapsed on him.

"Please, Franco."

"Come, ride on me." He helped her straddle his thighs, tugging her panties to one side to expose her wet center. He stroked her clit, and she jerked in response. "Oh, yes, you're ready for me."

She found the strength to push up and then, with his fingers guiding his engorged shaft, sank deep onto his full length.

They both cried out. He pulsed inside her, and she couldn't help spasming around him. He groaned. "Do that again."

She squeezed her little muscles again. He stroked her clit at the same time and she started to come again, panting and moaning on him as his dark eyes glittered with triumph.

She finally caught her breath. "Darn you, Frank, I wasn't ready."

"Your body thought otherwise." He began thrusting

up into her, his powerful hips easily leveraging their weight.

"But I've never come so fast—not at the tree, and not like this."

"Good." If she thought he was triumphant a minute earlier, he looked positively savage. "You are mine, and only I can make you feel like this." He caught her waist in his big hands and lifted her up and down until she caught his rhythm. He was heavenly inside her, slipping up and down until she could feel every glorious inch of him, stretching and filling her.

He moved his hands to her satin-covered bottom and squeezed the tender cheeks. "I would like to see you on my motorcycle like this—did I tell you I have a big American motorcycle at my estate in Portugal? I would start the engine and put you on the seat wearing panties and my leather jacket."

Julia groaned. She'd never seen motorcycles as being particularly sexy until today. "Then what?" she whispered.

"Then I open the jacket and play with your pretty *tetas*." His long fingers stroked her breasts, going from her collarbones down to where he cupped their full weight. He teased and pulled at her nipples until they were long and diamond-hard, darkened with excitement. All the while, he pistoned in and out of her. Her panties tugged and rubbed at her bottom as his cock brushed her clit. The constant pressure and friction was arousing her to a fever pitch. It was easy to imagine the erotic motorcycle fantasy since Frank still wore his tight T-shirt and dark jacket. Seeing him still clothed while she was almost naked was a huge turn-on, as if she'd ripped off her own clothing and the bare minimum of his, just to have her way with him.

Which was mostly true.

"Tell me what you want, Julia. I will do anything to please you, to satisfy you." Frank's deep, sexy voice continued, his accent thickening as he fought to keep from coming. Drops of sweat beaded on his temples and ran into his thick hair.

"I want you to talk to me." His words were almost as arousing as his body.

He laughed. "I like to talk. Nice weather, eh?" His teasing expression told her he knew exactly what she wanted.

Her face heated. "Talk dirty to me, Frank." Her bluntness was rewarded by his groan.

"Oh, Julia, if you knew the things I want to do to you, you would run screaming."

"Or maybe come screaming," she panted.

He groaned again. "You asked for it." He pinched her nipples again. "I want to lick you here." He stroked her clit. "And here. And all over your pale, soft body. I want to tie you to my bed and make you scream in pleasure. I want your hot, wet mouth to suck me dry and then lick me until I harden again and beg for more."

Julia started to shake, her mind and body reeling from his physical and verbal onslaught, but he wasn't finished. "I want to make love to you in my house in Portugal, in my barns, my stables, my vineyards, my motorcycle, my truck, my car. Everywhere I go, I want my cock to harden as I remember how I entered you, how I pleased you. I want to remember the sound of our damp skin slapping together as I enter you, the scent of our joining, your face as you come."

He continued murmuring to her in the soft consonants and liquid vowels of his native language, but the images he'd planted in her head were more than enough. She tossed her head back and cupped her breasts, playing with her nipples. He called out his appreciation and caressed the sensitized nub where their bodies joined. His shaft pumped inside her, hitting deeper than ever before. He kneaded her bottom, his heavy balls tightening against her, rising up to meet her.

"Ah, Julia, please..." he begged, the tendons in his neck standing out as he strained to hold back. Suddenly, she wanted his mouth on her breast and leaned forward. He eagerly captured the hard point between his lips and nipped.

The painful pleasure snapped her tenuous control and she exploded around him, her inner muscles capturing and squeezing him from root to tip. He called her name in a hoarse voice as his orgasm hit and slammed up into her, his hands gripping her around the waist as he pumped in and out of her eager body, slick and wet and as on fire for her as she was for him.

It seemed to last forever, but ended too quickly. He helped her ease off him and tucked her into his side.

Julia couldn't help admiring his still-firm erection, dark and glossy with their juices. What would it feel like the next time? She stopped herself—she was getting too greedy for him. All his talk about bringing her to Portugal and sexing her up silly at his estate was just talk—although she would have liked to try the motorcycle. She would like to do all the things he wanted her to do, in all the places he wanted to do them. Her greedy flesh gave an unexpected throb at the idea and she shivered.

He noticed. "Cold?"

"No." She laughed. They were both sweating, despite the cooler air under the trees. He was *still* hard, and his fantasy about licking him clean until he was ready to go again seemed very plausible.

A car passed on the road below, and she stiffened in alarm. "What if someone comes up here?"

He listened for a second, and then relaxed when the engine passed. "We are quite safe." His gaze fell to her half-naked body, her nipples still hard and tight. "Although *you* may not be. I hear there is a sex-crazed duke wandering the islands, and he absolutely loves dark-haired beauties with perfect breasts and round, white bottoms."

"Oh, Frank." She pushed at his chest, inordinately pleased that he thought she had perfect breasts. As for the round, white bottom, well, she'd take that as a compliment, too. "If the duke gets caught naked in the woods, there might be a royal scandal."

He laughed. "It has been a while since you lived in the Azores. I am a young, single man and can get away with almost anything. You've heard the phrase 'Boys will be boys'?"

"Yes." She wrinkled her nose. She'd always disliked that phrase, as well.

"The islanders would gossip if we were caught, of course, but they know a beautiful, sexy woman is staying with me on my island. I bring her to lunch and they see for themselves how I can't keep my hands off you. It would be no surprise to them that I drag you into the woods and have my wicked, ducal way with you." His erection, which had been fading, started to rise again.

She was getting excited again too. "Your Grace,"

she teased, "I believe your wicked ways are showing again."

"You're right." He shifted to his side and pulled her underneath him. "You make me insatiable, and I am going to take you again." He settled between her thighs, his cock nudging aside her panties.

He entered her without asking, and she caught a glimpse of how his ancestors must have seduced and plundered their concubines. If they had been anything like Frank, those young women must have been as eager as Julia was to surrender.

Her knees fell open and his thrusts were excitingly slick from their previous encounter. She couldn't help responding to his possession of her body and wrapped her legs around his waist.

He stopped and hooked her knees over his shoulders, changing the whole angle. Her bottom was up off the ground, their bodies where they joined blatantly revealed.

"Frank," she whispered.

He shook his head. "No, I want to see how you take me in. I want to see your soft pink petals turn rosy with lust. Already, I can see you swell and throb." He stroked around her clit, never quite touching her there.

"But, Frank…" Her protest fell off as he pressed her clit. "Ohhh…"

He laughed and slowly pumped in and out of her. "You want me to take you. You want me to hold you as my captive. You came to my island just for that, knowing I wouldn't let you go once I had you again. You brought an overnight bag, knowing that you would willingly submit if I took you that night. Your body rules you now—and my body rules you now."

She gave a little gasp, knowing he was right. His lazy, measured strokes were igniting a fire in her that only he could quench. And since he'd just climaxed, she knew he could go a long time.

"Say it," he coaxed, brushing her nipple with a feather-light touch. "Don't worry about being a modern, independent woman. Admit that you want me to make you respond like you never have before."

"I admit it." She swallowed hard. "I know you won't hurt me, so I want you to do whatever you want. Wherever you want."

"Good." His sudden grin made her laugh. "You can come now."

Julia did, obeying the duke's command. He was as merciless as his ancestors must have been, his hips pumping into her as she shook and cried out in ecstasy. His cheeks were dark with barely restrained lust, his eyes glittering black but he only paused to lower her legs to the blanket.

She took a deep, shaky breath as he slipped from her. "But what about you, Frank?" He was obviously still aroused to a fever pitch.

He gave her a sly smile. "This is the second part of my motorcycle fantasy." He helped her to stand and walk over to the motorcycle. "Face the bike and rest your hands on the seat." Julia's eyes widened as she realized what he wanted to do but couldn't resist the crazy idea, couldn't resist him.

She did as she was told and she felt his strong thighs rasp her bottom as he positioned himself behind her. Big hands pulled her leather jacket open and cupped her breasts, and his thick, slick cock entered her again.

He hissed in pleasure and began slamming into her,

his fingers teasing her breasts, her clit, her bottom. He nipped her earlobe, licked the side of her neck. Incredibly, she tightened with pleasure again—after three climaxes.

He pushed deep inside her, hitting the perfect spots with his tip. He was a masterful lover and Julia couldn't get enough of him.

"I'm such a brute to use you this way," he murmured into her ear. "Tonight I'll run a hot bath for you and carry you to bed. Let me kiss you all better—all over."

She groaned. Frank's lips and tongue on her pulsing, sensitive flesh sounded like a dream come true.

He laughed. "All you'll have to do is lie back and enjoy it. All you have to do is come under my mouth…"

"Frank…" The syllable trailed off into a scream as her strongest climax yet broke over her. Her nails dug into the bike seat and she pushed back into his luscious shaft. He gave a harsh shout and exploded into her, pumping frantically as her body rocked around him. Her nipples rubbed the leather as her breasts swayed. Her whole body trembled in pleasure as she braced her hand on his rock-hard thigh.

He eased them down so she lay in his arms on the picnic blanket.

"Are you all right, Julia?" His brow creased into worry. "Was it too much for you?"

She stretched, feeling nothing but a welcome fatigue. "I feel wonderful, and if we didn't need to ride farther on that bike, I might have you do it all over again."

His face broke into a grin. "Insatiable wench." He kissed the top of her messy hair and took a long, leisurely stare down her body. "I think I need to buy you some black leather clothing of your own."

Naughty images of Frank wearing motorcycle chaps and nothing else popped into her mind. "Only if you get some for yourself."

He wiggled his eyebrows. "I already do."

She decided to change the subject. "I didn't expect your friends to be so nice to me, especially the women."

He gave her a strange look. "Why ever not? You are a nice person, they are nice people. Most everybody here is friendly."

"Yes, but…" She wasn't sure how to describe it. "The local Duke sleeping with an American woman."

"Somebody said that to you?" Frank's face darkened.

"No, Frank, nobody said anything. Nobody even gave me a funny look." But she bet his mother and sisters would have had something to say if Frank had ever brought her home to them. Eleven years ago, Julia had been too young and naive to manage well in such a foreign environment, and now…maybe she was too old and jaded.

"Are you sure?" He was still wound up for battle. "Because I won't tolerate anyone insulting you. Not here, not anywhere."

Wow. She knew he had a protective streak but had never seen it directed toward others on her behalf before. "I'm sure. José's family was lovely, and they adore you."

He relaxed a bit and grinned. "And I am sure as soon as we left, they were on the phone to fill in Benedito back home. He keeps better tabs on me than my mother ever did."

"From what you've told me, it sounds like you needed it."

"Maybe when I was younger, but now he would

definitely be in the way." Frank stretched and rolled out from under her. "As much as I hate to say it, we should get dressed and go."

She gave the dappled green clearing a wistful look before reaching for her clothes. Their little Eden would linger in her memory for a long time.

"Such a shame to cover yourself up." He shook his head mournfully. "That is why I want to get you back to Belas Aguas so we can be truly alone."

Julia stopped in the middle of dressing. She was an expert on being alone, an expert on loneliness. Being alone with Frank was a misnomer—the time they spent together, just the two of them, was everything, the perfect connection with another human being that she'd longed for and never thought she'd have again.

She cupped his cheeks and kissed him sweetly, tenderly. "Thank you, Franco. Thank you for everything."

He rested his forehead against hers. "I owe you more than I can ever repay."

She closed her eyes and sighed, her heart filling with the love she'd pushed away for so long. Her uncomplicated spring fling was certainly more complicated than she'd bargained for.

AN HOUR LATER, AFTER zipping along the road back to her parents' apartment, Julia unlocked their door and pushed it open, wrinkling her nose at the musty air.

"How are your aunt and uncle this week, Julia?" Frank glanced around the apartment to make sure it was still in one piece, checking under the sink for leaks and making sure the fridge was still running. "Is your aunt still in the hospital?"

"Oh, I forgot to tell you." She beamed at him and his

heart thumped. "I called Boston yesterday and they're both doing well. My uncle's broken leg is starting to heal nicely and my aunt is doing much better since her ribs stopped hurting so much. The home health nurses and physical therapists are visiting several times a week to make sure they keep up their strength."

"I'm glad to hear they're recovering. Have your parents set a date for their return?"

She found a bottle of orange soda in the fridge and took a sip. "Ah…all that motorcycle riding makes me thirsty." She winked at him and his heart flipped to see her dark curly hair wild over the leather jacket. "I don't think they can come back for a couple more weeks. Once my uncle can move more easily and doesn't need as much help with daily activities, my mom and dad will consider it. Anyway, my mom is grabbing the chance to visit some of her old friends and go shopping for new summer clothes. My dad has the keys to my condo so he's probably hanging out there just to catch a break once in a while. I have many TV channels."

When the topic of her father came up, Frank still got the same embarrassed feeling that he had when he'd been a teenager. Sure, he and Julia were adults, but once Frank had a daughter, he'd knock any man on his butt who looked at her like Frank looked at Julia. If he ever had a daughter.

They heard a tapping sound and turned. Her parents' landlord *Senhor* de Sousa stood in the doorway. Frank greeted him in Portuguese, asking how he was.

"Fine, fine," he replied, taking a deep breath as if climbing the stairs had taxed his strength.

Julia gave her neighbor a narrow glance that Frank

didn't understand. Was she angry at the man for stopping by?

But she invited him in and smiled at him, the wariness never leaving her eyes. "A hot day today, isn't it?"

Senhor de Sousa wiped his brow, which suddenly looked pale and clammy. "Yes, hot." Then he dropped his English and lapsed into gibberish.

"What? What is he saying?" Julia grabbed the older man and guided him to a chair.

Frank shrugged helplessly. "I have no idea. It's Portuguese, but a bunch of words that don't make sense."

She groaned. "Darn it, I thought he didn't look good when he came in." She held on to his arm. "Listen, Frank, call the ambulance right now. Tell them he's having a stroke and they need to call ahead to the hospital. It's a good hospital, right?"

"Excellent care," he assured her and ran for the phone. Out of the corner of his eye, he could see Julia talking slowly and carefully to her neighbor. She was doing some kind of neurological exam, moving her finger side to side and up and down in front of his eyes. She smiled at him and encouraged him to do the same, but even from across the room, Frank could tell that one side of his face was severely drooping. The older man could raise one arm, but not the other.

Frank finished giving instructions to the ambulance and hung up. "They should be here in just a few minutes. We're fairly close to the fire station."

"Come over here and help me steady him so he doesn't fall out of the chair." Julia had her hands on *Senhor* de Sousa's shoulders, part for support and part to soothe him.

Frank reassured the man in Portuguese and although

it seemed like forever, the emergency crews arrived. Julia told them what had happened, using Frank as a translator. He didn't understand half of it, but the paramedics did, and they bundled her neighbor off to the hospital.

"We should go too, Frank." Julia put her hand on his arm. "I have his daughter's phone number. You call her and tell her we'll meet her there."

"Okay." He called while Julia locked up the apartment and soon found himself back on the motorcycle again riding toward the island hospital, Julia behind him. Not what he had in mind for a romantic outing, but seeing her in action was impressive. If she hadn't had her nurse's training and education, if she hadn't recognized the signs of *Senhor* de Sousa's illness, he could have easily gotten worse, perhaps to the point of death.

Julia was a wonder, not just in her relationship with him, but in her chosen career, as well. Would she ever consider giving up the excitement and satisfaction of saving lives at the big city emergency room to stay with him? The Santas Aguas estate was usually pretty tame, aside from occasional cuts and broken bones that came with farm machinery and big animals. Thankfully there hadn't been a serious accident in several years, but he couldn't picture Julia hanging around the small infirmary waiting for a fieldhand with a barbed wire scratch to wander in.

And he wasn't sure if she'd enjoy the formal duties that came with his life back in Portugal. His mother had mentioned spending less time with her charitable events and obligations and spending more time with his nieces and nephews, but *somebody* from the Duarte family needed to be on the boards of the Santas Aguas women's club, Friends of the Library and the garden club. Frank sure wasn't going to offer.

On the other hand, Julia could offer classes in CPR and first aid to the local scouts. Exciting stuff. He sighed and flipped on the turn signal to enter the hospital parking lot.

He spotted the emergency room drive-up lane. So did Julia. She tapped him on the stomach. "Let me off here. I'll meet you inside."

Frank pulled over and helped her take off her helmet. She strode into the E.R. without looking back. He'd never seen this focused and driven side of her until she'd diagnosed poor *Senhor* de Sousa's stroke. She really was a marvelous woman, personally and professionally. He was a goner for her—always had been.

An impatient horn tooted behind him, and he realized he was blocking the driveway. He got out of the way, parking the motorcycle. He cut the engine but sat on the bike for a couple minutes, worrying about what to do. The woman he loved had given no signals about what she wanted to do after their little island interlude ended, as all good things did.

Leaving her adrenaline-packed life in Boston for a sleepy Portuguese burg in the middle of nowhere would be a huge sacrifice. He wasn't sure what her answer might be to that dilemma once he got up the nerve to ask her.

11

Fashionista Magazine: The Royal Review:

WHAT WEDDING DRESS HAS Princess Stefania chosen? That's the burning question for our readers (and the designers poised to create instant knockoffs). We at *The Royal Review* have heard some hints, but everyone, even our own beloved Countess Lily de Brissard, is exasperatingly mum.

Princess Stefania has confirmed that she's wearing a dress designed by her brother's ladylove, New Yorker Renata Pavoni. Renata, who just may be Stefania's sister-in-law someday, is known for hip dresses with a retro flair. A trip to her website at Peacock Designs shows white, pink, ivory and even black-and-white dresses, full skirts and heaps of crinolines. Perhaps our modern princess is going for a vintage vibe?

Whatever the princess chooses is sure to be a trendsetter for upcoming brides. Renata, a stunning redhead who has kept infuriatingly quiet about her reportedly steamy relationship with

Prince Giorgio, told us, "It's always been my goal to offer fun, beautiful dresses for brides. Every woman is a princess on her wedding day. Stefania is so beautiful—she's a dream to dress. But you won't see her wedding gown until her groom does!"

THE NEXT MORNING, JULIA heard a car horn toot outside her parents' apartment and hastily zipped her duffel bag. Frank had arrived to take her back to Belas Aguas after their unplanned overnight on São Miguel.

Despite his claim that she could go naked on his island and he would be perfectly happy, Julia wanted more clothing for variety's sake. They still hadn't discussed how long she might stay, but once her parents came home, her libertine carousing was done.

A knock sounded at the door. "Julia, *meu bem,* it's me," Frank called.

She opened the door and pulled him into her arms, her hands roaming over the soft dark blue cotton of his T-shirt.

"Hey, hey." His startled laugh was cut off by her passionate kiss. His lips moved sweetly over hers and he backed her into the apartment, kicking the door closed behind her. She finally let go of him and he lifted his head. "Not that I'm complaining, but what was that for?"

She ducked her head, suddenly shy. "I'm just glad to see you."

"And I'm glad to see you, too." He caressed her cheek with his strong thumb. "Did you miss me?"

"Well, yes." She gave him a mock grumpy stare. "You could have stayed here last night."

"No." His tone was uncompromising. "It would embarrass your parents to have the single Duke of Santas Aguas stay overnight unchaperoned in their apartment with their single daughter. I wouldn't dishonor them that way."

"Oh, Frank," she scoffed. "Who thinks about that nowadays?"

"We Portuguese do. Do you want the neighbors gossiping about your parents?"

"No, but they know I'm staying at Belas Aguas with you."

"Out of sight, out of mind. Even if the neighbors comment on that, and I'm sure they do," he added dryly, "your parents will know that we had enough respect for them and their home to behave properly there."

It was sweet to consider her parents' feelings and reputation, even if she had tossed and turned all night without him. "How was the hotel?"

"Lonely." His mouth pulled down. "And since we were at the hospital until after midnight, they had to put me in a broom closet of a room next to what sounded like the main water pipe for the whole building. It roared any time a guest brushed their teeth or flushed the toilet."

"Oh, poor Franco." But she couldn't stifle a giggle.

"Yeah, I can tell you're all broken up about it." He picked up her duffle bag. "Maybe we should just head for the island instead of to the surprise I have planned for you."

"Another surprise? You don't have to do that if we need to return to the villa."

"As much as I enjoyed our trip to Furnas yesterday, several hours at the emergency room last night were not what I call the perfect ending to a perfect day. I'd like to make it up to you."

"Okay, then." Julia was willing to be talked out of a day of painting over deep red paint splotches. She locked the front door and made sure it closed tightly. Without *Senhor* de Sousa to keep an eye on things, she would have to rely on mechanical theft deterrents. "Frank, we should call the hospital before we go…wherever we're going. I want to know how *Senhor* de Sousa is doing, but I wasn't sure if anyone there spoke English."

"I already stopped there this morning after I traded the motorcycle for the car." He held her elbow with his free hand as they descended the outside stairs. "He is doing about as well as they can expect, but the doctor told me he has excellent chances of nearly full recovery. Your quick reaction allowed them to almost totally dissolve the clot in his brain and prevent further damage."

"Oh, Frank!" They were on the sidewalk now and she threw her arms around his neck. "How wonderful!" She planted a big smooch on his cheek. "That's exactly why I went into emergency medicine—saving lives and making a difference."

"Of course." His smile seemed a bit strained, and she felt guilty for tooting her own horn thanks to someone else's misfortune.

"But I wouldn't have known what was going on without you telling me he was speaking gibberish in Portuguese and being able to call the ambulance so quickly."

He put her bag in the backseat of the loaner car, a white compact. "I can call the hospital later since you will want to follow the progress of your patient. But he's in the best of hands at the hospital, so you can put your mind at ease." He opened the passenger door and settled her into the seat.

"Thank you, Frank."

"No thanks necessary." He went around to the driver's side and started the engine.

"Where did you say we're going?"

"I didn't." He grinned at her and acted as a tour guide, pointing out various historic churches and government buildings as they cruised across town. The scent of flowers floated into the car on a gentle breeze stirring the morning air. She sighed in happiness.

"Are we going back to the park for more pastries?"

"Pastries and kisses?" he teased.

Her face heated and she swatted his thigh. He covered her hand with his. "Not here, *meu bem*. I have to concentrate on my driving."

"Frank!" She yanked her hand back and crossed her arms over her chest.

"You can distract me later." But the traffic did thicken as they passed through the crowded center of town, braking for pedestrians and reckless drivers as they went.

"This is the road to the airport. Are you trying to get rid of me?"

"Nope." But that was all he'd say despite her pestering him the rest of the way into the airport parking lot and finally the terminal.

He stopped in front of the counter that listed that its next flight was to the island of Terceira. "Terceira!" she squealed. "Frank, I haven't been to Terceira since I was a kid." That island, about ninety miles from São Miguel, was home to a small joint Portuguese–U.S. Air Force base where her dad had been stationed for a couple of years. The Azores had been an important refueling pit stop for transatlantic flights ever since the 1930s.

Their flight to Terceira on a small commuter plane was short but slightly bumpy. Fortunately Julia had taken more airplane rides than ninety percent of the population and wasn't fazed at all. She did enjoy holding his hand, even if she wasn't nervous.

They touched down smoothly on the runway and within a few minutes were driving away in a small rental car. "The airport's much different than I remember—they've remodeled it since we were last here."

"Nothing stays the same," Frank told her. "Not even my villa on Belas Aguas that was firmly stuck in the past, décor-wise."

"Benedito did his best to update that. And we still need to tackle his Experiments in Red, kind of like Picasso's Blue Period. Or maybe not."

He groaned. "Oh, yes, he's just too avant-garde and hip for a stuffy aristocrat like me."

Julia laughed. "You just can't appreciate an *artiste* ahead of his time."

"Here's the base entrance. Would you like to see if they'll let us drive onto the base?"

"That would be wonderful." After being thoroughly vetted from their driver's licenses and the rental car inspected top and bottom, the base's guards gave them a temporary pass and let them through.

Julia eagerly scanned the base, recognizing some of the older buildings. "They've added a new hotel and I think that office building is new." Her eyes started to sting at being back at one of her childhood homes. She'd had so many and had never returned to any of those air bases, a typical military kid. "Oh, Frank."

"I know, I know." He patted her knee. "That office building is ugly enough to make you cry. Why, oh, why can't they find good architects?"

She burst into laughter at his attempt to cheer her. The office building was really ugly, but she was so used to military architecture that she barely noticed. "I'm glad you brought me." She wiped her eyes.

"I've been to Terceira before but not visited the base." Frank looked around in interest. "This is a little American town in the middle of the Azores. Some of the houses look kind of Azorean, but the rest is solidly American."

Julia pointed to the green hills behind the base. "And that is solidly Azorean. But the American airmen and the Azorean townspeople get along very well."

"Just like you and me." Frank pulled over near a small playground where preschoolers swung and climbed. "A good mix of America and the Azores." He took her hand. "Have you thought any more about visiting me at my ranch?"

Julia bit her lip and immediately let go, but he'd spotted her nervousness. "Yes, I have thought about it and it sounds fun." That was an understatement. "But I still have my job back in Boston. I've been gone quite a while already and I need to go back as soon as I'm able."

He pressed his lips into a tight line. "I know you love your work, but it's dangerous. You're the perfect example of someone who is only trying to help people and gets terribly injured. You could have been killed."

"I'm not ready to give up my work." *It's the only thing I have,* she almost said. She took a deep breath, realizing that wasn't true. She had her family and her friends. And now she had Frank. She looked out the car window at the children, screaming with glee. "But I will think about coming to the mainland to see your estate. It sounds lovely."

He grinned at her compromise. She wasn't very good at compromising, so she must have startled him. "It is lovely, sunny, warm and dry almost year round. At the top of one of the hills you can see twenty miles in all directions, the land spreading out below you like a brown-and-green quilt."

After a long, cold Boston winter, *sunny, warm and dry* was magic to her ears.

Her stomach growled and Frank laughed. "Can I bribe you further with lunch?" He started the car and drove away from the playground.

"Yes, but let's go off base for that. The restaurant here specializes in cheeseburgers and sandwiches, and I'd like to try the local food."

He agreed and they finished their driving tour of the airbase. Julia made a silent vow to visit some of the other places she'd lived as a child. She'd parked herself in Boston for years and not traveled out of New England, maybe as a reaction to moving so often when she was younger.

Frank drove out of the gates and toward the town. The village was crowded for a weekday, and they finally slipped into a parking space on a side street.

"I wonder what's going on today." Julia looked up and down the sidewalk. Young men laughed and jostled each other while the young women pranced along the uneven sidewalk.

"Must be a festival." Frank spotted an older woman selling fruit drinks from a cart and started chatting with her. He broke into a grin, his white teeth flashing.

Julia raised her eyebrows when he returned, excitement pulsing through him. "What is it?"

"There are going to be bullfights throughout the day and everyone is welcome to try."

"Bullfights?" Julia had a hazy memory of her dad warning her to stay away from them.

"Not the Spanish kind, *meu bem,*" he reassured her. "The Azorean kind where the bull doesn't get hurt. Just a little bit annoyed." He laughed. "Annoyed bulls—my favorite kind."

"You're not thinking of fighting them, are you?"

He waved his hand dismissively. "It's not a fight— more of a taunt."

She shook her head. "You have to be crazy to consider it."

"I know what I'm doing and I'm sober, unlike most of the guys here. Besides, you're not the only one with a taste for danger."

She pursed her lips like a fussy old lady.

"Oh, the look on your face." He pulled her into his arms and kissed her tight mouth. She relaxed grudgingly and he gave her one last kiss before letting her go.

"I just don't want you to get hurt, Franco," she told him, using her pet name for him.

"If you think I want to get gored or stepped on, think again. Hard to make love to you with broken ribs," he murmured seductively.

"You do know how to charm an emergency room nurse," she said wryly. "Maybe they're finished for the day?"

"No, they usually bring three or four bulls and rotate them."

"Great."

He laughed and hurried her down the street. "Come on, you'll like it."

The street was barricaded to traffic a couple blocks later, leftover cardboard tied to protect decorative railings. Julia realized that was so the bull couldn't stick his horns through and possibly gore someone.

Spectators perched on high walls and grassy areas. "This is where they bring the bull? This tiny space where you can't even fit two cars across?"

"This is it." His eyes were sparkling and he spotted an empty space behind a fence. He boosted her over despite her increasingly loud protests. "Stay here unless the bull's coming at you."

She called his name but he waved and trotted toward the large wooden pen at the end of the street. Someone set off a firework rocket and the bull exploded out of the pen to the cheer of the crowd.

The bull was glossy and black with blunted horns, a rope knotted around its neck. Julia's gaze followed the rope to see four or five men in traditional flat-brimmed hats and white long-sleeved shirts holding the other end. She hoped they knew what they were doing. And that the rope held.

Frank let the other men on the street dart close to the bull and then sprint away as the animal wheeled to chase them. He was probably gauging the bull's reactions and temperament. After a minute or so, he was in the thick of it. Julia bit back scream after scream as he ran toward the bull and circled away at the last second. Once he even affectionately touched the angry animal's snout, almost as if it were his pet.

"You maniac," she muttered, her nails digging into

her palms. He probably did this at home at his *fazenda* for fun, minus the rope.

A younger man, probably still a teenager, slipped and went down right in front of the bull. Frank was there in a flash to distract the animal, grabbing both of his horns and yanking him away so he was forced to step sideways. The bull snorted in anger and tossed his head, lifting Frank off his feet and bouncing him back down on the ground. That time she did scream, a short cry she muffled with her hands. She wouldn't forgive herself if she distracted him and he was hurt. Or even killed.

For a second Julia thought he would slip under the bull's hooves, but the men holding the rope pulled the bull back just enough for Frank to vault past the bull like some kind of circus acrobat.

The crowd roared its appreciation for Frank's bravery and fine bull-handling skills. He gave a cheerful wave without glancing around, still focused on that damn bull.

If he hurt Frank, Julia would make him into hamburger.

Now that the bull was wearing out, some of the older men took their turn and Frank gracefully stepped back.

He came toward Julia and easily leaped up to where she gripped the fence. "What did you think, *meu bem?*"

"Franco Duarte, you just took ten years off my life with that stunt. If you think I'm going to—mmmph!" She broke off as he grabbed her and kissed her.

A cheer went up around them as he claimed her mouth, claimed *her,* with his blatant, masculine power.

Julia yelped and he took advantage of her open mouth to deepen their kiss, his tongue teasing hers briefly.

Her fingers crept into his dark, silky hair and she pressed against his hard chest. Now that he was out of danger she could admit that watching him challenge the dangerous animal had excited her.

She ran her hands down the strong shoulders and arms that had lifted him safely around the bull.

He lifted his head with a jerk, realizing they had an audience. Julia caught someone murmur "Duke of Santas Aguas," and Frank grinned ruefully. "My secret bullfighting identity is blown. If only I had a cape."

She laughed at his joke, and he pulled her into his side to greet the people around them. As always, he was friendly and cheerful, introducing her as *Senhorina* Julia, who had lived on the air base as a child. That made the local Terceirans even more appreciative and it was several minutes before Frank and Julia could move toward a quieter part of town.

"That was crazy. *You* are crazy." Julia shook her head.

"I told you I'd done this before." He raised their linked fingers and kissed her knuckles. "I know bulls."

"You're full of bull," she accused him. "But you saved that boy from being trampled, so I forgive you for putting me through that."

"Thank you, *meu bem*. I'll treat you to lunch to make up for scaring you."

"And dessert." She wasn't a pushover.

"Certainly. I booked us a hotel room here so we wouldn't have to hurry back to São Miguel for the night."

She smiled. "Hopefully our room is far from the main water pipe."

He brushed her cheek with his fingers. "I made sure of it."

TWO DAYS LATER, JULIA stretched in bed, the early morning light reflecting off the mercifully taupe walls. Frank was gone, but he never went far. They'd worked hard getting the master bedroom back into a civilized appearance.

The smell of coffee wafted upstairs and she smiled to hear his baritone humming get louder. He poked his head around the bedroom door and grinned when he saw that she was awake. "Good morning, Sleeping Beauty." He carried in a dark wooden tray with two steaming cups and pastries on a plate. He wore his customary khaki shorts and unbuttoned white linen shirt that showed off his rich, dark skin.

She checked the clock, which had been flipped over at some point last night. "Nine o'clock? Why did you let me sleep so late? We have work to do." She sat up in bed and wrapped the sheet around her.

He made an exasperated noise and carefully set the tray on the bed next to her. Rich pastries with powdered sugar and jellies made her mouth water. "Work, work, work. We have done the most important job, which was to cover up Benedito's awful experiment in color selection. The new mattresses and bedding are on their way and fortunately the floors are stone and not covered with wall-to-wall pink carpet. Everything is good." He handed her a thick red-and-blue pottery cup. "Drink."

Julia accepted gladly. He had put exactly the right amount of cream and sugar in hers, which made her heart swell a bit. His coffee was deepest black, but she knew it always sweetened up a bit thanks to his habit of dipping a corner of his pastry. "If you don't want to work today, what do you want to do?"

His significant expression made her pink up a bit. "Besides that, Frank!"

"What?" He gave her an innocent look. "I thought we could go to the beach on this beautiful sunny day."

"The beach," she mused. "I haven't gotten much sun lately."

"You see?" He pointed a pastry at her. "Good for your Vitamin D and your mood, correct?"

"Are you saying I'm moody?"

He held a pastry up to her mouth and she took a bite. "You are always in the perfect mood for me."

She harrumphed but bit off a piece of…yum… pineapple-filled Danish. "Okay," she said, once her mouth was empty. "You've talked me into it."

"Great. We'll pack a lunch and eat at that little cove south of here. Swim, sun, whatever we want." He settled next to her on the bed and chatted to her about weather patterns on the island, migrating birds and whatever he found interesting and thought she might, too.

It was soothing and domestic to watch him drink down his coffee and gesture with his pastry as he strewed crumbs across their bed. Almost as if they were an old married couple that had settled into an easy morning routine. She had never had that with a man before.

"More coffee?" He pointed at her empty cup and she shook her head.

"I should get up and get ready."

"What's to get ready? Go to your bathroom and put your suit on."

"Frank…" Really, he knew better after having four younger sisters, five if he counted Stefania.

"Fine." He heaved a sigh and gathered the plates and cups. "I'll be downstairs ruining my hands in the dishwater if you need me." The kitchen had a perfectly functional electric dishwasher.

"Your hands are fine."

He winked and hopped out of bed. "That's what certain people tell me."

She chucked a cabbage-rose pillow at his head and he darted out of the bedroom, roaring with laughter. She couldn't stop giggling as well as she dug out her swimsuit and headed for the bathroom.

FRANK HELPED JULIA OUT OF the heavy-duty golf cart as they reached the dune above the beach. "Go down to the water. I'll bring the supplies."

She slung her totebag over her shoulder and stepped into the sand, her white linen cover-up blowing in the breeze. Belas Aguas had beautiful soft white beaches, unlike some of the other islands that had dark, volcanic sand or rocky coasts. The sand was cool and damp against her feet as she sunk into the top few inches.

Frank had packed enough gear to cross the Sahara instead of one small Atlantic beach, so she left him to it and picked her way down the dune to the water's edge.

She stopped and stared at the horizon. Straight south of them was…nothing. Just cold seawater, until the ice of the South Pole. She shivered, not quite knowing why that bothered her. She quickly turned east, taking some comfort that Portugal and Africa were there, if thousands of miles away.

Frank came up next to her. He wore an unbuttoned cream cotton shirt over snug black swim shorts, a light dusting of dark hair highlighting the smooth tan skin underneath. "That's the problem with island living. You look out to sea and think, 'Here I am, alone on this rock, with nothing but water and birds around me.'"

She turned to him. "You feel that way, too?"

He wrapped his arm around her shoulder. "I told you I don't come here often. Maybe that's part of the reason—it makes me morose."

"You? You're so sunny and cheerful."

"I have my moments, like everyone." He kissed the top of her head. "Here, sit." He unfolded a low-slung beach chair and settled it into the sand. "I have to set up the cabana."

She craned her neck. "You brought a cabana?"

"Of course. We always bring one so my mother and the kids can get out of the sun. My mother is deathly afraid of sun damage and wrinkles and the kids get fussy unless they can lie down to rest in the shade." He knelt in the sand and unzipped a white equipment bag, pulling out what looked like a mass of poles and matching white fabric.

"Do you need help? That looks complicated."

"Super easy." He extended several poles and quickly raised a square-topped, open tent as if it were a giant umbrella, hanging weights from each pole. "All I have to do is put on the sides and we're good."

Out came more white fabric and he snapped three sides to the top frame until they had a cozy little tent. He unrolled an area rug and set up a couple more chairs inside. A small portable music player, food cooler and side table followed.

"This looks like a sheik's desert palace. Is this where the dancing girls come prancing in?"

He grinned. "Are you volunteering?" He took off his shirt and stood in front of her in only his short shorts.

"Maybe later." She winked at him.

"Too bad." He pouted. "I'll be here if you change your mind. Or maybe I can change it for you."

"You probably could," she muttered. "You're very persuasive."

"Only with you, Julia."

He had said that before. Despite the fact that he was one of Europe's most eligible bachelors and probably had women fling themselves at him regularly, she believed him. "Thank you, Frank."

"No need to thank me for the truth." He beckoned her into the cabana. "Here, come put your things inside and have some sangria."

"Yum." She didn't resist when he poured her a mix of red wine and fruit juice, full of chunks of pears, apples and oranges.

"Not too much, though," he cautioned. "Sun and wine can be a potent combination. I don't want you to get a headache."

"And I don't want one, either." She settled into a lounge chair. "I haven't had one in several days, and I sure haven't missed them."

"You see? The Azores are healing you—you should extend your stay."

She shook her head and laughed. "You're incorrigible." More likely it was Frank's presence healing her. Ever since she'd come to Belas Aguas, the weight that had been sitting on her chest had lifted, only settling back briefly if she thought too much about what would happen when it came time for her to leave.

But it was too beautiful today to worry about that, even though she was a world-champion worrier. Frank lifted his glass of sangria in a toast and they clinked glasses.

She set hers down in the sand and yawned after she finished the sangria. "Let's get into the water before I fall asleep."

He was up on his feet before she finished her sentence, tugging her up from the chair. "First, you have to ditch the cover-up. I want to see your suit."

She grabbed the hem and slowly pulled it up and over her head, enjoying his sharp intake of breath as she revealed her yellow string bikini.

"Swimming's canceled." He hustled her back into the cabana and made as if to close the front flap.

She wriggled away from him and dashed to leave.

He caught up with her in seconds and together they hurried down the beach and ran into the ocean hand-in-hand.

Julia screamed as the cool water splashed up around them. "Franco!" She hopped from foot to foot until either she adjusted to the temperature or went numb.

"Sorry, Julia." He didn't sound apologetic at all. "This is the Atlantic, not the Caribbean." He bent and splashed seawater up at her and she kicked some at him in return.

"Frank, I'm getting goosebumps all over," she complained, crossing her arms over her middle.

"I happen to like your goosebumps." His gaze was focused on her breasts. Even through the light padding in the bikini, her nipples were visible peaks. He caught her around the waist and pulled her in close. Her legs automatically wrapped around him. "And can I tell you how much I like your bikini?"

"I can tell you're sincere." She wiggled against his erection, the biggest proof of his sincerity.

"Oh, I am sincere." His fingers played with the nape of her neck. "Can I tell you how much I sincerely want to take your new bikini off?" He pulled the neck string and the yellow triangles were floating between them. "Very nice." He stroked his fingers down her neck to her collarbone and then across the plump upper curves of her breasts.

"I float."

He laughed. "Easier for me to reach." He cupped each breast, his thumbs gliding over her wet nipples to tease them into hard peaks.

She arched back and enjoyed his warm hands playing over her. The water supported her weight so it was almost as if she were floating in midair. The water didn't feel so cold anymore against her super-sensitized skin. In fact, she wouldn't have been surprised to see steam rising from the ocean around them.

He dipped his head and captured a nipple in his mouth. She yelped in pleasure and grabbed his shoulders to keep from sinking. He found a side tie to her suit bottom and loosened it, finding her own wetness underneath.

She almost went underwater at that point, but he let go of her breast and braced her again. "Ever wonder how mermaids make love?"

"Why don't you show me?"

He found her clit, circling and petting it. Occasionally

the cool water swept over her, making her shudder in delicious shock. He kissed her lips, her cheeks, her neck, flicking her earlobe with his tongue.

"Oh, Franco." She sighed, closing her eyes. It was perfection being in his arms under the warm sky. He murmured her name and kept touching her until she clutched at him, her climax pouring over her in a giant wave. He anchored her to the ground but let her fly toward the sun in pleasure.

He gathered her into his arms and carried her out of the water toward the cabana.

"Put me down, Frank." She dropped to her knees in front of him in the sand, her fingers hooking over his waistband, the scrap of black fabric begging to be released. So she did, pulling the wet material down to his knees.

He caught her shoulders but couldn't move his legs for fear of tripping. "Julia, wait…"

She was eye-to-eye, so to speak, with the pride of the Dukes of Santas Aguas. They must have been a virile bunch, if Frank was any indicator. "Good grief, Frank. However did you get all of that in your suit?" He was hard and thick, pearly fluid rising from him like foam on the seawater.

He gave a choked laugh. "I wasn't like this when I put it on. Now come on, stand up."

"No." She sank onto her haunches and resisted his efforts to raise her. "Stop fussing, Frank." His outraged squawk turned into a groan when she put her mouth on him. His skin was cool and salty from the ocean, quickly warming as she swirled her tongue around him.

She lifted her head and smiled up at his face, pulled into taut lines.

He broke then, kicking his suit free and picking her up as she squealed his name. He carried her toward the tent, but she stopped him. "No, here."

"On the beach?" He gave her a sly smile. "Between the woods and the beach, you're turning into a real nature girl." He set her on her feet and grabbed a blanket out of the cabana. He tossed down the blanket and tugged the corners to smooth it.

Julia untied the rest of the bikini strings and lay down next to Frank. "You're so beautiful." She stroked his face, and he actually started to blush.

"Men aren't beautiful."

"You are." She rolled onto her back, the sand soft under the blanket. "Make love to me under the sun, Franco."

He swallowed hard and moved on top of her. "Julia, open for me."

She eagerly did, and he slid into her. His thrusts were hard and possessive, making her gasp with pleasure. She tightened down on him and he groaned, his skin turning slick with sweat.

"Come with me, Julia. I can't wait much longer." He balanced his weight on one strong arm and stroked her sensitive nub again. She wrapped her legs around his waist and rocked with him, becoming one with him. His fingers teased and caressed her, and her climax built again. He noticed and thrust harder.

She cried his name as she came. He groaned in relief and followed, the sounds of their pleasure swirling in the air like the calls of the seabirds.

Frank rested his head next to hers, his breath still choppy and fast. Julia kissed his cheek and stared up into the sky. This was pure perfection—if only life

could be like this forever. She shoved her worries away,
determined not to let them intrude again as she held her
wonderful man in her arms.

_12_

THE DREAM CAME AGAIN THE next night, the first time in the two weeks she'd been with Frank. Julia knew she was in their bed back in Belas Aguas and knew she was only dreaming. But she couldn't stop it, couldn't wake herself. She was crying in her sleep at what would come.

It hadn't started out as anything but the typically drunk patient on a Saturday night in her Boston emergency department. He had come in for stitches for a scalp wound—nothing serious, but it looked as if someone had bashed him due to the bruising around the wound.

He'd only mumbled something about standing up under an open kitchen cabinet when she'd asked him what had happened. She had her doubts but he was a large guy, definitely big enough to take care of himself. His dark flannel shirt was covered in dried blood. His chart said his name was Mark.

She'd numbed his wound and prepared it for suturing, her needle ready to close the edges. She probably wouldn't need most of the suture kit, which included several different clamps and a scalpel.

Julia inserted the needle into his scalp, trying to line up the edges of the skin as neatly as possible. He twitched. "Did you feel that?" He might need more local anesthetic.

"No, just do it."

"Okay, but let me know if it starts to hurt." She moved along the wound, knotting and cutting the threads.

She focused on her work but noticed Mark getting more and more agitated, twitching from side to side and breathing rapidly. He didn't flinch when she poked him, so it wasn't pain. Was he mentally ill?

Through an opening in the privacy curtain, she caught sight of Lyle, the retired cop who worked as a security guard in their emergency department. She jerked her head slightly in her patient's direction and Lyle's still-sharp instincts made him amble casually in her direction.

Lyle stuck his head in the room. "Julia, how're you doing today?" His broad Boston accent always made her smile, but she was getting a weird vibe from her patient. Lyle was, too. He came into the room, his tan uniform pressed neatly and his silver hospital security badge shining on his chest. "How are you tonight, sir?"

"Gotta get out of here!" Mark jumped off the bed and jerked away. Julia yelped, her thread still sticking out of his head with the needle dangling in his hair.

"Easy, buddy," Lyle tried to soothe him, thumbing his radio for back-up.

Julia tried to get out of his way but the agitated man grabbed her wrist. "Help me, Lyle!" she yelled. She vaguely remembered him tossing her away from him, her head cracking into the corner of the countertop.

When she opened her eyes next, she was on the floor, her head splitting in pain. Lyle lay near her, blood pulsing from his chest. He was pale and clammy, losing blood at an alarming rate. The patient stood about ten feet away, a red-stained scalpel in his hand. The scalpel from her kit. He must have grabbed it after shoving her and then stabbed Lyle.

Julia brutally forced back the pain, pushing up to a sitting position. "What are you doing?"

"I've had a rough evening." He laughed nervously. "Any minute now, the cops will be here for me."

What did he expect? A mint on his hospital pillow?

He read her scorn. "Oh, yes. But what you don't know is that he's not the only person I stabbed tonight. Caught my wife cheating. Tonight she grabbed a knife and well, I got to her first." He swallowed hard. "I didn't mean to, but she wouldn't stop screaming at me about her stupid boyfriend. I had to shut her up."

"Don't make this worse for yourself," she stated as firmly as she could. "Put down the scalpel and let me help the guard." Other staff were yelling in the hall for help.

"Get back or I'll finish them both off!" He shrugged. "What's one more murder tonight? I'll get life in prison whether it's one life—or many."

Julia went cold. Lyle wouldn't make it if he didn't get medical help soon, and she was pretty sure she had a bad concussion.

Sirens sounded in the background, distracting Mark. He looked away briefly, and she caught sight of a small ankle holster above Lyle's heavy black shoe. She never would have seen it if she weren't sitting on the floor.

Non-regulation, but the guard was a retired cop and probably never went anywhere without a gun.

She crawled toward the guard. "Please, let me help him." She clutched at his leg, unsnapped the holster and pulled out the small black revolver. She pointed it at Mark's middle. "Drop the scalpel!"

"Now where did that gun come from?" He sounded more interested than intimidated, and that was more frightening than rage. He was a man with nothing to lose, holding her and a dying man hostage with a deadly weapon in the middle of the emergency department. He moved toward her.

"Get back!" Her vision split him into two and then back into one. But the scalpel was her focus.

He waved it so it glinted in the light. "You're as bad as my *late* wife. My *late* wife. My dear, departed, unfaithful wife." His laugh echoed crazily. "Put the gun down and I won't kill you."

No, her father's voice floated in her mind. *Don't. He's lying.*

"I know," she whispered.

He grinned, blood trickling down his face and growing bloodlust in his eyes. The first murder might have been an accident, but she feared he was beginning to enjoy himself. "That's a good girl. Gun's getting heavy for a tiny thing like you, isn't it?"

It was.

"And you don't even know how to use it, do you?"

But she did. Her father had taught her in the pistol range when they lived in the Azores. Oh, Azores. Oh, Franco. If she failed, she would never see him again.

Thumbed back the hammer, the click deafening in the small room.

His eyes narrowed. His shoulders bunched. He was coming.

Her finger tightened on the trigger. God help her.

Aim for center mass, her father commanded. *Start shooting. Don't stop until the gun's empty.*

He came.

She obeyed her father. For once. And he saved her life.

Julia sat up in bed with a scream.

"Julia!" Someone grabbed her around the shoulders and she screamed louder. She was immediately let go. "Julia, please! You are safe."

She opened her eyes and saw Frank kneeling next to her. "Oh, my God, Frank. I am so sorry. Did I wake you?"

His eyebrows shot up even higher and she realized what a silly question that was. But he didn't point out the obvious. "Julia, are you all right?"

"Fine." She pressed her hand against her thumping heart.

"No." He rested his hand on her knee. "Sometimes you cry out in your sleep, but nothing like this. What is your nightmare, Julia?"

She sighed. "I lived it a few months ago when I got hurt."

"What?" He sat next to her and gathered her into his arms. "You told me you hit your head at work and got a concussion. Does that give you nightmares?"

"In a way." She took a deep breath and told him about the man coming into the emergency room needing stitches. How he had grabbed her, slamming her head against the wall and stabbing the guard. Frank listened silently but his distress grew as she told how the man had killed his wife.

"I grabbed the guard's gun when I fell next to him and scooted away from him. The bad guy came at me and I shot him."

Frank gasped. "You shot him? You?"

Julia almost didn't believe it herself. It had been something out of a cops-and-lawyers TV show. The cops had just arrived. The first one on the scene yanked her out of the room, the second aimed his gun at the dead man.

Her savior dragged her around the corner and took the gun from her hands. The emergency team rushed in for poor Lyle as soon as the second cop called the scene clear. "Are you okay, miss?"

The floor wobbled under her feet, and he called for help, supporting her weight. "You did good, miss."

It was a good thing to kill someone?

The cop read her unsaid question. He was in his forties with a ruddy, lined face and weary, though kind blue eyes. "He would have killed you, too. You get to go home tonight. He doesn't."

With her concussion, she didn't go home that night. But she did go home.

It was still very raw, but she'd come to see the older cop had been right. "Yes, he had a scalpel and would have killed me as well as the hurt security guard. I had to do it to save us both. And we both survived. Lyle needed surgery and lots of blood tranfusions, but the last I heard, he was doing well."

"Thank God you did what you had to do." Frank's voice thickened. "Or you would have been lost to your family. Lost to me. How could we have gone on without you?"

She touched his forearm. "Frank, you haven't seen me in eleven years before now. You went on without me for that long."

"No, I didn't." He pulled her against his strong chest, her cheek resting in the springy hair. He stroked her head. "I didn't go on, Julia. I went back to New York that August and was a mess. George and I went out to a bar and I got drunk and cried in my beer. I told him some of what had happened between us, he dragged me home and poured me into bed. He's the only one who knew about us."

"I was a mess, too, Frank. I went back to school and slept-walked through the first semester, waking up only when my grades took a nosedive."

He gave a melancholy laugh. "I wouldn't get out of bed for my classes. George dragged me into the university counseling office after I missed the first week. It helped me cope, but not much more. Portuguese dukes are not good at taking suggestions. Arrogance and anguish are a bad combination."

"I had to go to a counselor a couple weeks after I got hurt," Julia blurted out. "They said I was at high risk for post-traumatic stress and made me visit the police psychologist, of all people."

"Why him?"

"Her. Because she knows what to say to people who have just shot criminals." Julia nudged him in the side. "That's typical of you to assume it would be a man." Her effort to lighten the topic made him grin.

"Julia, my love, you of all people know I would never underestimate a woman."

"*That* guy did."

He actually growled. "I am glad he is dead, Julia, because I would kill him myself for daring to hurt you. My darling." He kissed her forehead.

She allowed herself to sink into him, to let him comfort her. Although her parents had tried their best after the shooting to help her through the trauma, she had purposely hidden her distress to protect them and their feelings. Looking back, she probably hadn't fooled them at all, especially her dad, who had lost several Air Force buddies to warfare, training accidents or airplane crashes.

"Come, lie down with me again," Frank coaxed, fluffing her pillow and covering them up with the soft cotton sheet and summerweight blanket. "I'll keep you safe. Don't worry, *meu bem*."

Julia rested her cheek on his chest. His heart thumped under her ear, fast but slowing gradually as they relaxed. She drifted back to sleep, knowing somehow that her dream wouldn't return that night.

FRANK STARED AT THE CEILING, forcing himself to breathe slowly and steadily as to not alarm Julia. Julia, his Julia, forced to face down a deadly criminal and kill him herself. None of this, not one bit of this would have happened if he hadn't been such a coward after they'd parted. He'd taken to his bed like a melancholic poet instead of chasing after her.

He'd handled their break-up poorly, but in his defense, twenty-year-old men were not the most polished creatures. And he'd lost more than only Julia.

He'd let her sleep, let her dream more pleasant

dreams. And in the morning he'd make it very clear
that he wouldn't make the same mistake of letting her
go again.

THE NEXT MORNING, FRANK had something on his mind,
Julia could tell. She'd fixed him *chouriço* and pancakes
topped with honey and pineapple jam again but he'd
been unusually quiet. She wondered if he was thinking about her nightmare last night. "More coffee?" she
offered.

He shook his head. "Let's go for a walk."

Julia looked out the window at the gray clouds scud-
ding along. An Atlantic storm was blowing in, but she
was used to them. "Promise me we'll head back before
we get blown to the mainland."

"It won't take long." He handed her a slicker and put
one on himself.

She didn't quite know what to make of that but it
sounded as if he wanted to have a relationship chat. Not
what she was looking forward to, but inevitable. Her
life and career was back in Boston, and his was at his
Portuguese estate.

She suppressed a sigh and walked out the kitchen
door in front of him. They crossed the stone terrace
and descended onto the lush green lawn.

The lawn ended at the rocky cove near the boat dock,
but he kept going over the rocks until they were out of
sight of the house, a raised bluff at their backs and the
ocean at their feet.

"We never did talk about why we broke up eleven
years ago," he said.

"We've talked about the past somewhat, Frank. Why
do we have to dwell on it?"

"Because our problems lie in the past." He took a deep breath. "We both remember why we broke up back then."

Blood rushed to her face. "A misunderstanding."

"You were pregnant, Julia." His expression was as serious now as it had been eleven years before. "And then you weren't."

"Shut up, Frank!" It burst from her before she could stop. "Just…stop." She really didn't want to discuss this. They'd never discussed this. "It doesn't matter…it was only a couple weeks that we knew about…that."

But he battled on. "I'm so sorry you lost our baby, Julia. I could have handled it better."

"Yes, you could have."

He shrugged helplessly.

"I was about a week pregnant, looking at two little pink stripes on the dipstick, and you put your hand on my shoulder and told me we would get married in the fall."

"Obviously! I couldn't leave you to face it all alone. Did you think I would just jet back to New York to school and let you explain everything to your parents without me to support you?"

She'd been careful to keep her miscarriage secret from her parents at first but had broken down and told them later in the year after they'd found her sobbing in her room one day. "I was your obligation, and you never once mentioned love, just marriage and duty."

"But you *were* my duty."

"And I was scared to death. To drop out of school, to marry you, to become a mother. I would have been the nineteen-year-old pregnant Duchess of Aguas Santas.

I'm sure your mother would have loved planning our shotgun wedding."

"She would have loved it, because I loved you. And now we are older and hopefully wiser."

"I don't know about wiser, Frank. We seem to be repeating the same pattern."

He looked down at her, his expression ironic. "Well, I don't want to break up again. That part doesn't bear repeating. If you didn't realize I loved you eleven years ago, I'll say it again—I love you still. And I hope you love me, too."

"Oh, Franco." She cupped his smooth jaw. What was she going to do? At least she could tell him the truth, no matter what she decided. "I don't think I've ever stopped loving you."

He wrapped his arms around her. "I'm so glad to hear that. If I hadn't been such a fool, we would have been settled at my estate long ago, and you never would have been put in such a dangerous position. Forced to take a life to save your own."

"Of course I regret that, but I don't regret the other parts of my life." She regretted that he had never knocked at her dorm room door, that she hadn't taken the train to New York to find him at his apartment.

"Not at all?" He raised a black brow.

It had been a second-best option, but the best one she'd had at the time. "I got to finish my education, get my nursing license. I graduated from graduate school with high honors. I've met so many patients and their families, had the chance to help them live, and some of them, to help them die. I don't regret that at all."

"It doesn't seem like a fair trade," he informed her.

"Losing our baby and a happy life with me for sick people you don't even know."

She pushed out of his arms. "I don't need reminding about the baby, Frank. I cried every day for months and had to go to grief counseling to even function. I don't think it was a fair trade because life is not fair. We don't get a certain number of points to redeem, and if we lose the tickets, we aren't given another packet. Why me? Why not me? Do you know how many young people and even children I've seen die? They have parents, too, and none of us is spared pain and suffering. Not in this life." The cold, damp wind blew strands of hair across her face, temporarily blinding her. She brushed them out of the way.

His jaw jumped. "Then forget about that. I insist you come to Portugal and marry me. I can give you another baby—I can give you as many as we can manage. You don't have to waste your emotions on strangers."

He still didn't understand. Her schooling and career was the only thing that had saved her from despair and paralysis. And his second proposal of marriage was about as grim as the first. She told him so.

"Well, excuse me if I am doing this wrong," he replied sarcastically. "But I have only done this once before and it seems that I'm not doing any better this time."

"We don't have to get married. Why don't we just get together in Boston or I could even come to Portugal to visit? Maybe not right away since I have to go back to work next month and I've been on disability leave."

"What? You're going back to work?"

"My work means a lot to me."

"So come work in Portugal. You would learn the language easily and there are plenty of hospitals."

"It would take me months, if not years to pick up Portuguese well enough to function in a high-pressure work situation." And then what? Date Frank on her days off? Live with him at the *fazenda?* Marry him and be the Duchess of Santas Aguas, hobnobbing with royalty and presiding over a huge estate?

"I think I know what is going on. When you work at the hospital, you can be the most caring person around—but only temporarily, and only on the surface."

"What?"

He nodded. "I understand why, because you would not be able to function if you cared deeply and permanently about your patients. Maybe you are carrying that over to me—to us."

She frowned at him.

"Julia, this is our life. You don't have to protect yourself from me."

"Yes, I do." She spoke without thinking, but it was true.

"Why? I know I hurt you before without meaning to, but now things are different."

"No." She backed away from him. "You love me too much and you want too much from me."

"What?" He ran a hand through his damp black curls in frustration. "Why is that a bad thing? I don't understand."

"I can control things at my job—or at least deal with them better."

He gave a bitter laugh. "Oh, yes, things are so much under control that you had to shoot a murderer in your emergency department. And you would rather go back there than stay with me?"

"Yes, because that was just physical pain. If my heart broke again, I wouldn't be able to survive." If she lost another baby, that would be the end of her. Guess that grief counseling hadn't worked so well after all.

He dropped his hands to his sides. "And that is that, eh?"

"Yes." Julia tipped her face to the sky, hoping the rain would disguise her wet cheeks. She'd been a fool to think she could spend so much time with Frank, spend so much time making love with him, and not encounter heartbreak. But maybe she could minimize it if she got away from him. "When can you take me back to São Miguel?"

His shoulders slumped. "Back to your parents' apartment?"

She nodded, and he looked out to sea. "After the storm. Unless you want to get away badly enough to risk the weather." He sounded bitter, and she didn't blame him.

"I'll pack and we can leave when it clears." She turned to leave him. "I am sorry, Frank."

He faced her, his eyes shocking in their desolation. "Don't apologize, Julia. I actually feel sorry for you— that you would give up a second chance at our love just because of fear. I have never known you to be a coward, but people do change. I know I have." He looked over the ocean again, and she left him. Left him to pack, left him to go back to her predictably unpredictable life of long hours at the emergency department and long hours alone at home.

Maybe that would sound better once she got back

into her usual routine. And once again, she would never drive to the Azorean enclave south of Boston. Because the locals there would wonder why the sight of Portuguese pastries and smoked sausage made the American girl cry her eyes out.

BENEDITO HUNG UP THE PHONE in the main kitchen of the estate of Santas Aguas, his lovely wife Leonor chopping vegetables for dinner.

"Well?" She selected a potato and diced it like a machine. Leonor with a knife was slightly frightening, but Benedito knew how to keep on her good side.

"The duke has royally messed up."

She snorted. "He let that girl get away from him?"

"Again." Benedito nodded. "And he wants me on the next flight to São Miguel to help him finish the renovations."

Leonor pointed the wicked-looking blade at him. "That boy will never marry anyone but that American girl. And he will never marry her unless he sees her again. Don't you want little Duartes running around the estate? Putting them on their first ponies, teaching them about the long, proud traditions of our land and our people?"

"Of course, woman!" he barked. "I did my best to bring them together this last time, but now the Duke will throw himself into this renovation, and then it will be time for Stefania's wedding. He will be in Italy, for goodness' sake."

Leonor stopped slicing, her gaze faraway. "The wedding. Invite her to the wedding."

"But I don't have the power to do that." He spread

his hands wide. "You and I are going, but we can't take her as a guest."

"Not us, *idiota*. Call little Stefania. She will do anything to make Franco happy."

"Ah." A wide grin spread over his face. "*Meu bem,* you are a genius." Making sure the knife was set down, he threw his arms around his wife and kissed her. "As always, you know exactly what to do." He lowered one hand to her ample bottom and gave her a pinch.

She squealed, but all that did was press her delightfully full bosom against his chest. He wiggled his brows. "Hurry up with that chopping. As soon as I get off the phone, I will show you my appreciation."

"Oh, you." She shoved him away, but her face was flushed. Benedito cackled and found the battered phone book with Stefania's private number and dialed. First, the phone call. And if dinner was a little late, too bad. He had to make the most of his time with his voluptuous wife before answering the ducal command to return to the Azores.

13

"JULIA, YOU HAVE MAIL." A peculiar tone in her mother's voice made her get up from the couch where she was pretending to read an old mystery novel she'd found in the island's English bookstore. No more romances for her, novel or otherwise.

It had been two weeks since she had seen Frank. Julia had returned to her parents' apartment in São Miguel, and they had very kindly not barraged her with questions about what she'd been up to while they were gone. The neighbors had surely filled them in. She'd caught her parents giving her concerned looks, but she'd been careful to cry quietly at night or to just let the tears run down her cheeks while in the shower.

Frank was back at his *fazenda* on the mainland. She missed him terribly. He hadn't told her he was leaving. A much-improved *Senhor* de Sousa had said the Duke had stopped at the hospital to wish him well before he returned to the mainland.

The Duke hadn't stopped to wish Julia well. She'd caused enough turmoil in his life—again—that he probably just wanted to get the hell away from her. She really needed to get her head on straight.

And she was supposed to be back in Boston in another week or so—back to the craziness of the emergency room and the boredom of single life.

"What is it?" She padded into the kitchen and saw her mother holding a large ivory envelope.

"For you. The return address says, 'His Majesty Crown Prince Giorgio of Vinciguerra.'"

Her dad got up from his chair to peer at the envelope through his wire-rimmed reading glasses. "No street address, though. I suppose when you rule a whole country, people know where to send your mail."

"Why would the Crown Prince of Vinciguerra send you mail?" Her mother held on to the packet with a death grip as she practically fondled the expensive paper.

"Let her open it, Evelyn, and then we'll all know the answer to that question."

Julia didn't want to take the envelope. Prince Giorgio was Frank's best friend and the brother of the bride. It sure wasn't an invitation to a royal wedding shower. She couldn't even afford a cloth napkin off that bridal registry.

Dad tugged it out of Mother's hands and passed it to her. "Open it before your poor mom passes out from curiosity."

Julia slid her finger under the flap and pulled out a smaller, but no less exquisite envelope, this one addressed in beautiful calligraphy to "Miss Julia Cooper."

Inside was an invitation to the wedding of the decade, Princess Stefania to the star German soccer player Dieter Thalberg. And Julia had painted their honeymoon bedroom a nice relaxing taupe color. They could thank her later.

She handed the invitation to her mother, who gasped as she read. "How on earth did you get invited? Have you ever met any of these people?"

"Evelyn, it's because of that Portuguese boy. The one who turned out to be some upperclass dilettante."

"Frank is not a dilettante. He is well-educated and a hard worker," she told her father more sharply than she intended.

He gave her a satisfied half-smile, as if she had confirmed some hypothesis he'd been mulling.

She glared at him for tripping her up.

"Julia, you should go," her mother announced. "It's the opportunity of a lifetime, something you can tell your children about."

Fat chance of her ever having children. She didn't even want to look at another man who wasn't Frank.

"Don't be silly," her father scoffed. "Julia, at a royal wedding?"

The women both rounded on him. "What does that mean?" Julia demanded.

"Come on, now. We're regular people. They're royalty. All those fancy outfits and us in our T-shirts and shorts. Julia would probably curtsey to the butler—they have several apiece, you know."

Her mother was turning the color of a pomegranate. "Bob, that is the most ridiculous thing I have ever heard. You act as if we're some know-nothings who eat cold pork and beans straight from the can. That we think toilet water swirls around in a bowl. In all your years in the Air Force, did we ever embarrass you at formal functions? Did you ever see me with my skirt tucked into the back of my pantyhose or with my finger up my nose?"

"Now, Evelyn…" He held up his hands in placation.

"Good going, Dad," she muttered. Of all the things to bait her mother with—her mother came from a poor family and had worked hard to learn proper etiquette for all situations.

"Don't you 'now, Evelyn' me!" She waggled her finger at him. "Julia is going to this royal wedding and she will know exactly how to behave and you—you are treating her to a fabulous dress."

"But what if I don't want to go? I have to get back to Boston," she complained, sounding like a whiny teenager. She was just starting to come to terms with the idea of not seeing Frank again, and now her mother was tossing her at him.

Her mother put her hands on her hips. "Julia, you can just call up the hospital and tell them you're not ready to come back. You're still having headaches and you toss and turn at night."

She didn't realize her mother knew that. "I'm just tired," she said feebly.

"A good reason to delay your return to work. After all, you deserve a medal for being wounded in the line of duty. Your spot is as good as reserved," Dad informed her. The twinkle in his eye made her wonder if he had purposely goaded both of them.

"And you're paying for her plane ticket!" Mother announced. "And mine, too, because she and I are going shopping—in London."

JULIA CLUTCHED HER INVITATION as she stood in the guest line at the massive Vinciguerran cathedral. The facade was a warm ivory color with a huge stained glass circular window over the wide doors. A spire climbed upward, and Julia could see tiny figures moving around in its bell tower. They were probably preparing to ring the bells after the ceremony.

Most of the guests around her were obviously the rich and wealthy from all over Europe. But there were a few regular people like her wearing wide-eyed expressions of excitement mixed with terror at being so far out of their usual setting. She wondered if they were friends of the family or maybe former nannies or teachers.

Julia didn't feel any more comfortable, but at least she looked the part. Her mother had taken her to Harrod's and several other boutiques in London to find just the right outfit. She had fallen in love with a peach-colored hat with a slightly rounded crown and turned up brim. For decoration, it had a lighter-peach satin ribbon band and satin roses on one side. They had found a matching peach-colored suit with a low-cut V-neck and a skirt that hit right above her knees. Her mother had suggested in front of the saleslady that Julia might want to wear a lace camisole underneath, but had received such a look of horror from the clerk that she had immediately dropped the idea.

Julia wasn't interested in covering anything up. She wanted to rub Frank's nose in what he was missing. The peach color made her lightly tanned complexion glow and aside from feeling desperately miserable at not being with him, she looked great.

She was next in line, and got wanded by the security guard, her purse searched and discreetly sniffed by the police dog. Once that was done, she was directed to the cathedral entrance.

She climbed the white marble steps and blinked as she entered the church. Once her eyes adjusted to the lower light, her jaw dropped. Fairy-tale wedding didn't even come close—this was heavenly. The altar was pure ivory marble with large golden candelabras. Big swags of cream and yellow roses draped over every available surface, with smaller bundles of blooms attached to each pew.

"Bride or groom?" Julia looked up into the face of a Germanic god—not Odin, one that had both his eyes. This guy was blond, blue-eyed perfection and didn't even make her stomach quiver one teensy bit. She sighed and told him she was there for the bride. He checked her name and his eyes widened.

He extended his arm and she took the impressive appendage. Again, nothing. She didn't even wonder about any other appendages he might have as they walked down the aisle.

She hummed the bridal march under her breath and he gave her a mischievous look.

"Ah, the march from *Lohengrin*."

"Good job." Of course, he would know Wagner's greatest operatic hits.

"I'll see you at the reception?" His blue gaze traveled to her un-camisoled neckline.

"Me and nineteen hundred other people." She was just weary, too weary to even flirt with Handsome Hans.

He stopped at a pew close to the front and ushered her in. "Until then."

"Thank you." She sank into the gold cushioned seat next to a middle-aged couple that was practically quivering with joy. "Exciting day, isn't it?" It was time to get over herself and stop being such a hermit.

"But of course!" the man said. He was wearing what looked like a brand-new suit, his plump, pretty wife in a beautiful dress that had to be of French design. "We 'ave known the bride since she was small. I am Jean-Claude and this is my wife Marthe-Louise. How do you know Stefania?"

"I'm, um, actually a friend of Frank. The bride's Portuguese friend."

He translated for his wife, who'd suddenly become quite animated. "My wife, she says François is a wonderful man and is a brother to Stefania, her brother Giorgio and our own Jacques."

"Frank, George and Jack," Julia murmured to herself.

"Ah, *oui!*" Jean-Claude let out a laugh. "And Stee-vee, too."

She had been put in the family pew.

Then she saw him. He was walking down the aisle with an elderly woman wearing a tiara and perfectly draped silver silk formal gown that matched her hair.

He matched his pace to the older woman, so Julia had plenty of time to stare at him and try to keep her heart from beating out of her chest.

All the men were impeccable, but Frank was stunning. He wore what looked like a black military uniform, complete with medals and tons of gold braid. A red-and-white ribbon sash went diagonally from one broad shoulder to his opposite hip, where he wore a ceremonial sword with a jewel-crusted, cross-shaped hilt. His black hair was slicked back from his strong face and he looked solemn and serious, as befitted the occasion. But when he finally guided his charge to the front pew, she said something to him. He patted her hand and smiled, his joyous expression lighting his face.

Julia remembered that expression—saw it almost every night before she fell asleep. More and more, her nightmares were disappearing, replaced by dreams of being with Frank.

He returned to the front of the cathedral and took his place standing next to a tall, chestnut-haired man in equally elaborate regalia—probably his French friend the Count, the one with a baby on the way. She waited for the usual stab of pain, but it was only a slight twinge. Maybe she had been able to put more of that grief behind her than she thought.

A minute later, the handsome blond groom filed out from the side of the church to stand at the front of the aisle, his equally handsome blond groomsman at his side. The bishop and his assistants proceeded from the back of the altar. The bishop was regal in his pointed hat, shepherd's crook staff and white-and-gold vestments. He murmured briefly to the groom, who gave a nervous smile.

Music boomed from the organ and a pretty blonde flower girl started down the aisle, stopping on the opposite side from the groom.

The organist shifted pedals and started the bridal march. Everyone in the cathedral turned to face the entrance. A pretty, petite brunette smiled up at her brother, Frank's friend Giorgio. He was dark-haired and handsome, and even from the distance, Julia could tell he was fighting back powerful emotions of love and happiness for his sister.

The bride was so beautiful, Julia wanted to weep.

Sure, she had a wonderful ivory-and-gold satin dress and an antique lace veil streaming down her back. But the love in her face as she saw her groom was what made her radiant. The groom was dazzled by her beauty, his eyes wide and his mouth falling slightly open before he broke into a huge grin.

Giorgio safely delivered his sister to her fiancé and kissed her on both cheeks. She cupped his face in her small hands and said something to him that made him blink rapidly and swallow hard.

He nodded and kissed her again before standing next to Frank and their friend Jack.

The wedding was long and ceremonious, with several hymns sung by the local boys' choir and a hearty sermon from the bishop. Unfortunately, Julia didn't understand much Italian, but she understood the parts about love and making babies. Jean-Claude grinned and elbowed his wife at that part. Everyone was obviously thrilled about that aspect, looking forward to having babies to spoil.

What if she could have a baby with Frank? *Another* baby with Frank, she mentally corrected. She'd done her best to push the memory of the first one, the lost one, out of her mind for the past eleven years, but she'd come to see that was futile and unnecessary. She still loved that baby, just as she had always loved Frank.

If she'd learned anything about the human mind, she'd learned it was like a closet. Oh sure, you could cram all sorts of broken and damaged things in its depths, but eventually the closet door wouldn't close and everything would come bursting out.

She'd needed to stuff her grief into the closet in order to survive at first, but Frank had yanked open the door and insisted she clean it out. And he had grieved, too, poor Frank, with his tender heart and sweet nature.

Someone pressed a soft cloth into her hand, and Julia realized with a start that she was crying, streams of tears running down her cheeks.

The round face of Frank's friend Marthe-Louise creased in concern as she patted her arm. She seemed to know Julia was crying for more than just a beautiful wedding.

Julia wiped at her tears with the handkerchief. Marthe-Louise wrapped a sturdy arm around Julia's shoulders and a knot loosened under her sternum that she hadn't realized still bound her.

She forgave Frank for not chasing to Boston after her, she forgave herself for not chasing back to New York after *him,* and she forgave whatever unfathomable twist of fate that had taken their baby from them and wrenched them apart.

She knew now that she had come here not just to show Frank how hot she looked in her new suit, but also to start again with him. If he still wanted her. She'd certainly been difficult, turning his well-ordered life upside-down and sideways.

The bride and groom were exchanging rings and saying their vows, and her heart twinged. Frank might not want to try again with her—if they were on a sports team like the groom, their record would be 0-2. But maybe they could do a last-minute save.

Stefania kissed her new husband and a pleased murmur ran through the crowd. The happy couple turned down the aisle amidst the traditional organ music for the bridal recessional, grinning so hard their faces must have ached.

Julia turned her attention back to Frank. He stood and adjusted his sword, slapping Giorgio and Jack on the back. Giorgio whispered something in Frank's ear and he froze, the happy expression dropping off his face like a rock. He slowly turned and his gaze met hers across the pews. She hoped her eyes weren't red and watery anymore.

She couldn't tell what he was thinking, but she knew her own expression was equally stunned. Giorgio must have kept track of who she was and what she looked like.

Jean-Claude and his wife gave Frank a happy wave. He returned it absentmindedly, and understanding dawned on their cheerful faces. "Ah, you are a surprise for François, *non?*" Jean-Claude asked. "A beautiful surprise for him."

"Um, thank you."

"Not at all." They shook hands with her. "We see you at the reception, *mademoiselle.*"

Once the kind French couple filed down the aisle, Julia went the opposite direction, knowing that Frank would follow her and not wanting a big crowd watching them. A small chapel stood off to the side with a beautiful stained glass window of a golden dove in white beams of light.

Julia stared up at the window, wishing she could be so peaceful. Under better circumstances, she would love to sit here and try to relax.

She closed her eyes for a second, but knew exactly when he approached her. "Julia."

She turned. "Frank. Nice to see you." He was even more handsome close up, but his dark eyes were wary.

"I didn't expect to see you here, Julia."

"You didn't? I thought you asked the bride to invite me." How utterly embarrassing. And she'd even been put in a pew with his good friends. "But who did invite me?"

"Oh, Stefania did invite you—but it was probably that scoundrel Benedito who asked her. I made him quite miserable the week after you left."

"And this was your payback." She blinked hard, trying to estimate how quickly she could leave this pretty little country and run back to Boston. But she mentally stopped herself. Hadn't she done that once already?

"I made him miserable because I was missing you. He probably thought he was doing me a favor."

"Oh."

He moved closer, his sword and medals jingling. "How are your nightmares, Julia? I hate to think of you suffering. Sleep should be free of cares."

"They're fading gradually," she admitted. More and more often she dreamed of him instead, but that was a different kind of suffering.

"Good. I still feel terribly guilty for not protecting you from that sort of situation."

She exhaled impatiently. She had shopped till she dropped in London and had come across Europe for the same disagreement? "We already talked about this, Frank. I was a teenager and you were twenty. Neither one of us had a college degree and I'm sure your family on their private island and grand estates would have been thrilled to marry you off to the daughter of an American Air Force noncommissioned officer who didn't even own a home since we moved every few years."

"We Duartes are not in the habit of moving," he replied. "We haven't moved in eight hundred years."

"Will you move now?" she asked. "If I meet you in the middle."

"What do you mean?"

"I don't want to mess this up any longer. I can't stand not being with you. We survived the loneliness and pain and miraculously found each other again. What more can you ask after all these years?"

"Decades more." He pulled her to him and kissed her fiercely. He lifted his head. "I was an idiot to let you go. I could have easily found you but I thought you needed your space and you would eventually contact me again. When I didn't hear from you for so many months, I thought the memories were too painful for you to see me, so I gave up. We could have dated through college and married soon after, but I was foolish and stubborn, refusing to take the first step toward you."

"I was foolish and stubborn, too," she admitted. "I lived in my shell for so many years until I was almost shattered. I had to come to the Azores to make myself whole."

"I am not whole," he whispered. "Ever since you left me again, I am missing part of my soul. Come to me in Portugal, Julia. Marry me. As you Americans say, the third time's a charm."

"What?" She stared at him with huge eyes.

He dropped to one knee, heedless of his lovely uniform. "Marry me, Julia," he repeated. "Live with me in Portugal—make my estate a home for us. I cannot bear to be without you anymore. I love you with all my heart."

"Frank…" she murmured, stunned that he was

proposing to her again, here at someone else's wedding. Her mother would have a fit at the breach of etiquette.

"Do you still love me, *amor meu?*" He kissed the back of her hand.

"I do. I never stopped loving you for the past eleven years. Why do you think I never married, never even got engaged? My heart was always yours." She wrapped her fingers around his, shaking on her high heels.

"Then tell me yes, you will marry me. If you say no, I will crawl on my hands and knees following you around the cathedral. My sword will scratch the marble floors, my trousers will be ruined, and worst of all, my mother will berate me for acting a fool in front of all her friends."

Julia couldn't help giggling at the image. "Get up, Frank." She tugged at him, realizing they were attracting some attention. "Don't you know it's tacky to propose to a girl at someone else's wedding?"

He resisted her prodding easily. "Stefania will forgive me. She would be the first to cheer me on."

He was probably right. From all he'd told her, the bride was decidedly unconventional.

"I'm going to start singing Portuguese love songs in a few seconds," he warned her. "Three, two, one. *Te amo, te adoro, você quer casar comigo…*" His pleasant baritone voice echoed in the cathedral.

"Frank!" She slapped her hand over his mouth and he kissed her palm. He gave such a look of love from his sweet brown eyes that she melted. "Yes, I'll marry you."

He leapt to his feet. "Oh, Julia." Heedless of anything

or anyone around them, he pulled her into his arms and kissed her.

"Is that your sword or are you glad to see me?" she asked demurely.

He threw his head back and roared in laugher. "Both, of course. I'll unsheathe them for you later."

She groaned and rested her head on his shoulder. "Are you going to wear this for our wedding?"

"All of this plus the ducal coronet. It's family custom."

"Like a tiara?"

He gave her a pained look. "No, not a tiara—that is for women. A narrow gold crown for a man. And you get one, too."

"A crown?"

"A coronet belonging to the Duchesses of Aguas Santas. You'll be the newest."

She clutched his hand. "Your mother! Will she like me?"

"She'll love you. Would you like to meet her? She and my sisters are probably wondering where I am."

He'd been making more than enough noise to attract everyone's attention. "How do I look?" She patted her hat to make sure their kiss hadn't knocked it off. It sure knocked her socks off.

"You look like the most beautiful, the most precious, the most wonderful woman in the world," he told her. "And it is an honor that you will be my wife."

"The honor is mine."

He bent to kiss her again and a flash popped. "Uh-oh. I think the cat is out of the bag."

She giggled. "After we meet your mom, I need to call mine so she won't find out about us in the paper first."

"I'd loan you my phone, but I left it in my other ceremonial uniform," he said with a wink. Then his expression deepened, a look of awe and wonder on his face. "Oh, Julia, you have made me the happiest man in the world."

"And I'm the happiest woman in the world."

"I will never forget our past, Julia, but from now on, we only live in the present and plan for the future."

"Our future." She rested her cheek against his and smiled. A golden-white beam of light shot through the stained-glass dove and shone on them as a blessing. Their past had its dark moments, but they had finally come to a brighter place together. Forever.

Epilogue

Fashionista Magazine: The Royal Review:

LOYAL ROYAL-WATCHERS, we at *The Royal Review* would like to thank you, our wonderful readers for helping make our blog the most popular destination for royal news on the net, but we're not stopping now!

After the stunning wedding of Princess Stefania of Vinciguerra to soccer star Count Dieter von Thalberg, her brother Crown Prince Giorgio must have caught wedding fever. His office has announced the engagement of Prince Giorgio to American Renata Pavoni of Brooklyn, New York. The hunky prince met the stunning redhead when she was chosen to design his sister's wedding gown. It now looks like she'll be able to design her own wedding gown, fit for a crown princess.

This comes after the whirlwind wedding of Prince Giorgio's French friend, Count Jacques de Brissard to his lovely Countess Lily. Countess Lily has been kind enough to give us the exciting

news first—they are already expecting a boy
bébé—the next Count de Brissard! Countess Lily
says they will name him Henry Gérard—Henry
for her late father, and Gérard for the Count's late
father.

With wedding bells literally ringing, Prince
Giorgio's old college chum Francisco Luís Gus-
tavo Felipe Duarte, Duke of Santas Aguas, reportedly popped the question to his American
girlfriend, Julia Cooper of Boston—and at Princess Stefania's wedding, no less! A little birdie
tells us that she was the One Who Got Away many
years ago, so it's no wonder he didn't waste any
time recapturing the affections of the petite brunette. Looks like her nursing skills brought his
heart back to life! They have already set a wedding date for the end of August at the chapel at
Santas Aguas, the Duke's ancestral holdings in
the heart of Portugal.

The bride-to-be was overheard telling a gal
pal that the Duke had donated money for a new
hospital emergency room not only in the hospital nearest Santas Aguas, but also on São Miguel,
the closest hospital to his private island of Belas
Aguas. The part of this that will make you say
aww...the emergency rooms will be named in
honor of the Duchess Julia Cooper Duarte das
Santas Aguas. Rumor has it that the Duchess may
work part time there since she loves her work so.
Some brides get big rings, some get emergency
rooms—whatever makes your heart go pitter-pat!

So, alas, poor single ladies, three of Europe's
most eligible bachelors are eligible no more. But

you can be sure we'll bring you all the juiciest inside scoop for the upcoming weddings of Prince Giorgio and Duke Francisco. With all these happy couples, we'll be watching eagerly for the next generation to arrive!

* * * * *

Have Your Say

You've just finished your book.
So what did you think?

We'd love to hear your thoughts on our
'Have your say' online panel
www.millsandboon.co.uk/haveyoursay

- Easy to use
- Short questionnaire
- Chance to win Mills & Boon®
  goodies